THE ORCHID
AND THE FAWN

THE ORCHID AND THE FAWN

CHRISTOPHER DAVEY

SERENDIPITY

First Published in 2005 by
Serendipity
First Floor
37 / 39 Victoria Road
Darlington
DL1 5SF

British Library Cataloguing-in-Publication data
A catalogue record for this book is available from the British Library
ISBN 1-84394-140-6
Printed and bound by The Alden Press

This is a work of fiction: although all the locations referred to are (or
were) real places, all characters, except one, and events described are fi
tional, and any similarities to any real persons living or dead are purely
co-incidental.

This story is dedicated to Debbie, my Wife,
who taught me to care;
to Beth in Edmonton, Canada,
who committed my first draft to a floppy;
to Una Harrop – who believed in me;
to Jane Stuart;
and to all those – lawyers, particularly –
who persuaded me to see this project through;
and to Jersey Greyhound Rescue.

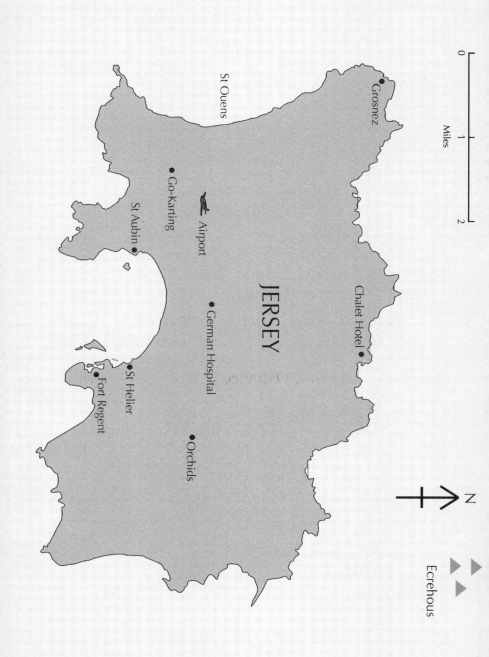

Contents

Prologue

The events to which this story relates happened some thirty years ago. The world has moved on. It is a less gentle place. I am not entirely sure that the same strengths of love and loyalty now obtain.

In this 21st century, Jersey, too, is greatly changed: many are richer, certainly, but that wealth gap has widened hugely between the local have-nots, who are doggedly 'hanging in' there, and the many immigrants who have, or have managed to acquire, so much. This story tries to celebrate, if only by implication, some of the quiet wonder that the Jersey tourist sought, found and loved about that little island back in the '70s, something that, even now, it is trying to recapture, as its people attempt to turn the tide on the politics of greed.

The school cane has been discarded long since.

Until paedophilia, always lurking in the background, suddenly reared its head in the public consciousness, consenting under-age sex with an older person had begun to be treated with an element of common sense – 'if he feels he's big enough, he's old enough' – and one might have believed that the distress so misguidedly brought down upon Helen, Sam and me could no longer happen under our slightly more enlightened justice system, where judges are younger and vicariously more aware of life as it is lived in the raw 'out there'. Yet I fear the pendulum may now be swinging back the other way. We were a very contented trio, harming no one: yet the law sought us out and crucified us. But for natural humanity and common sense intervening *against* such law, this story could have run yet more cruelly. Perhaps it *could* happen again ...

Writing about some of my most personal moments, and

examining publicly my feelings and emotions – even of long ago – has not been easy. Yet it has been essential, in order to get the story across. Helen has long wanted the story to be told. Sam too. I originally wrote it while I was a Cambridge undergraduate, but then laid it aside. It has been my Uncle Piers, now far gone in years, who has finally persuaded me to re-write and publish, feeling strongly as he does that all the facts *should* see the light of day.

I have avoided, so far as is possible, fictionalising this account – but if any readers, even after all this time, choose to identify times, places or people, they are at liberty so to do, but it might be helpful, nevertheless, if they kept such knowledge to themselves. I have had to guess at the detail of some of the scenes I describe, as even my Uncle Piers, whom I have turned to time and again since those terrible last days, was never able to elicit the whole truth of the matter.

My story, I believe, is not unique; but the impact of the telling of it may yet lessen the chances of such happening again.

M E H

CHAPTER 1

First Stirrings

There was this formidable thunderstorm. I normally sleep soundly, but even *I* was awoken by this one. I am forty-five now, but at the time of which I speak I was just ten years old, in a dormitory with seven other boys. In the flashing, banging and pouring rain, one of our number, it seemed, had fled down to Matron, and another had disappeared outside, while the remaining five were standing in their pyjamas excitedly watching nature's wondrous power from the windows. As I came awake I realised that they were all talking and pointing excitedly. "It's Nielsen," one of them shouted back to me through another crash. "Come and see what he has got!" I slipped out of bed and pushed my way through between them.

Outside, the lawn was lit up by the school floodlights. Sitting cross-legged in his dark green track-suit was this thin figure of a boy, unperturbed as the lightning flashed, the thunder rolled and the rain beat down. But the amazing thing was that, snuggled in his arms and across his lap, was a creature. Although he was in our dormitory, I knew Sam Nielsen only a little: he was skinny, with golden hair, creamy skin and piercing blue eyes. This little animal complemented him: clearly newly born, it was fawn-coloured and spindly, but with soft brown eyes. It was shaking and terrified. The boy, on the other hand, was not: utterly calm, he cradled it across his lap, stroking its quivering head.

"What on earth's he got there?" I asked.

"I know what it is," said one of the bigger boys. "It's a little deer!"

"Little dear!" I sneered. "Don't be so wet!"

"No, it is, it is; I saw one once. Promise."

I stared for a while, and then realised he must be right: it was a very young fawn that must have become separated from its mother in the storm, and fled out of the woods towards the lights.

All at once the boy outside got carefully to his feet, wrapped the animal around his neck and shoulders, walked towards our window and called up: "Hi, chaps, it's a bit wet out here and we're getting a tad cold. Just chuck us down my mac and some blankets, will you? Oh, and my pillow!"

I gave up one of my blankets and my own mackintosh as well, and we threw them down with the pillow off his steel bed. Then we watched in some awe as he wrapped himself up with the fawn and then bedded down on the grass in full view of all of us. As the storm ebbed away, we watched the pair fall asleep, and then returned to bed ourselves.

As dawn broke we got up and immediately looked out, but the lawn was deserted.

Nielsen was not at breakfast. "Where's Nielsen, Matron?" I asked.

She sniffed: "*Stupid* little boy! He was sleeping out on the lawn in the storm for a lark, and we couldn't find him. So thoughtless. Got us all really worried. I've sent him straight to the Head. He deserves a good thrashing …"

"But he was caring for that animal …" I protested.

"What a lot of nonsense! He was just playing 'Dare' in that storm: he could have got struck. And then where …?"

I did not wait to hear the remainder of her sentence. Without permission I had left the table and was running at top speed to the headmaster's study. At this time caning was the penultimate sanction, short of expulsion, in any headmaster's armoury. As I skidded to a halt, the oak door was closed, but I could hear the Head's raised voice inside: " … I am not sure which school rule you have broken, Nielsen, but if you have nothing to say, I judge that you have earned five strokes of my cane …"

I knocked on the door.

"Wait!"

I knocked again.

The door flew open, and the burly man was standing there, cane in hand: "I said Wait!, Hallam. Did you not hear me? Wait outside, and if you are still there when I have finished with this young miscreant, you will be next on the block!" With that he banged the door shut on me.

I was furious at the manifest injustice of what was about to happen. Through the door I could hear him inviting his victim to bend over the arm of the chair. I pushed open the door, entered and caught at the man's raised arm: "Sir, Sir, you mustn't do that: it ... it wouldn't be fair."

The arm was lowered and the figure turned towards me menacingly. He was livid, obviously, but curious too that one so youthful should challenge him so. "And why, pray, would it not 'be fair', as you put it? Go on, tell me, I would be interested to hear."

I faced up to him: "Because, Sir, he was out in that thunderstorm caring for this baby stag. Ask anyone, Sir; we all saw him do it. I promise."

Mollified, the man with the cane looked across at the boy who was shivering next to the arm of the leather chair, over which he had nearly been thrashed. The Head walked over and sat down in the next chair: "Sit down, both of you! Is this true, Nielsen?"

The little fellow nodded.

"Then why on earth didn't you *say* so, boy? Why didn't you speak up and say so, when I asked you? Think how *I* would have felt, had I subsequently discovered that I had thrashed you unjustly and without reason ..." He paused for a moment to let the selfish implications of this alternative act of criminality sink in.

"Sir, I don't know, Sir. I'm sorry, Sir. I s'pose I was just too scared to say anything," he stuttered.

"Humph! So, where is this creature now then, I wonder?"

Nielsen piped up: "Once the storm had gone, maybe she felt safe enough to go back into the woods, Sir, and look for her mother. But I expect she'll come back when she's hungry – if she can't find her mother, that is."

"Humph!" said the headmaster again. "Well, as you seem even to know whether it was a boy or a girl, I feel inclined to believe you. Go back to Matron, both of you, and finish your breakfasts! In the meantime I have an idea." As we left together, he was talking on the internal phone.

Along the corridor Nielsen suddenly stopped, took my hand, and shook it. His eyes gave me one of those piercing looks which I was to grow to love: "Thanks for doing that for me, Hallam! You were an absolute brick. My name is Sam; you can call me that, if you like."

"That's all right. Bit scary, but I bet I wasn't half as frightened as you. I'm Mark, by the way. But you have to stand up to grown-ups, you know: they can't be *always* right."

Of such, I suppose, are lifelong friendships wrought.

Nothing about the incident was said at Morning Assembly, but at break-time Sam and I were sent for. We knocked on the dreaded oak door, and it was opened silently. The headmaster was smiling almost mischievously: with his finger to his lips, he indicated to us to move quietly over to the window. Then he pointed down: there beneath the sill the little fawn was curled up next to an almost empty dish of milk. "Don't make any noise, boys!" he breathed. "Fawns shy at the slightest thing."

Suddenly Sam took off his shoes and socks. "Do you mind if I try, Sir?" He left the room, and in a few moments was walking silently across the lawn to the exact same spot as the previous night. He sat down cross-legged as before, and made an eerie sound. The fawn immediately looked up, then scampered across to where the boy was seated. He gathered her up, stood up, then indicated to us to join him.

The headmaster made another phone-call, and we then both went outside to stroke the creature, that, in the boy's arms, seemed completely at peace.

A minute later Matron appeared with her camera, and took some pictures, which were later to appear in the school magazine.

"Right, lads, back to class with you boys! Oh, and Nielsen, Sam, you were right, and I was wrong. And, Mark, thank you for having the nerve to come wading in when you perceived a wrong being done. Well done indeed! Showing a bit of guts in this world, particularly on behalf of others, is what life's all about."

The fawn became a regular sight, lapping her milk, on the lawn outside the head-master's drawing-room window for many weeks, until finally she disappeared back into the woods permanently. Sam Nielsen and I became, if only briefly, minor folk-heroes.

And, inevitably, we became 'best friends'.

Although we were the same age, almost to the day, Sam and I were complete opposites in every aspect. Maybe in consequence, we grew to enjoy each others' company in our free time and on the relatively rare occasions where our interests coincided. He was not very academic, but he had a pure singing voice; he played the recorder and painted, both with quite some skill, and made wonderful 'inventions' with his vast *Meccano* set. He often acted in school plays: I remember once watching him being nailed to a cross at Easter, and suddenly wanting to dash up and rescue him from the hands of the brutish Roman soldiers from the 6th Form, who were obviously relishing their roles. His creamy complexion and delicate frame always reminded me of that fawn he had rescued from the thunderstorm.

It was not until our third term at the school that Sam suddenly asked me if I would like to come out to lunch with him one Sunday. He had noticed that I was never taken out for Sunday lunch, because my home at that time was in Germany. I accepted gratefully. After morning church Mrs Nielsen arrived all the way from Suffolk in her little *Saab* car, and took us to a tiny restaurant in the next village. After the rather ordinary school food I thought it was an absolute feast. Afterwards we went to a swimming-pool, much better than our school one, where Sam showed off his prowess as a diver.

Then we had ice-creams. In all it was a wonderful day. I thought Mrs Nielsen was a really super mum, and when we got back to school I sat down immediately to write her a really long Thank-you letter. I also told my parents in another long letter – somewhat pointedly perhaps – what a wonderful day I had had with the Nielsens.

Thereafter, twice a term, Sam's mother would take us out for lunch on Sundays; each time we would explore a new restaurant somewhere else in the Cotswolds, afterwards voting it so many stars. With my own parents serving with the RAF out in Germany, Mrs Nielsen became a perfect mother substitute. My parents were both in their fifties, whereas Sam's mother was much, much younger. I really treasured these outings, never forgetting to write her a long letter afterwards to some place called 'Paradise Park'. Mr Nielsen was the racing driver son of a Swedish engineer who had developed his own racing-car construction business. His wife was always beautiful, serene, quiet and self-possessed, and never seemed to allow the worry and strain of her husband's career to show through.

A full boarding all male preparatory school is, and always was, the toughest environment for any boy to grow up in – for many, tougher by far, than any public school. Boys form into cliques, clubs, societies: for 'outsiders' life can be daunting. Sam and I formed our own private club, just the two of us: only reluctantly did we let others join us. Sooner, rather than later, they would drift away.

There was, however, one little boy, I remember, who seemed to be one of life's 'losers', short-sighted, stammering, useless at games, not much good at work, apparently not much good at anything really. His proper name was Graeme – I remember because he would always spell it out for people. But everyone just called him Twiggy. He was very thin, almost like a stick-insect, and one of the masters, when Graeme first arrived, had somewhat thoughtlessly asked him, in fun, whether he was related to the super-model currently in vogue – and the name had stuck. Sam and I felt rather sorry for him, and tried to include him in some of the things we did together. Initially Sam resented him, and I chided Sam: "Look, he's having a pretty awful time on his own, and he's harmless: let's at least *try* and be nice to the poor mut!"

And then Sam said a really nice thing: "OK, Mark, he must be good at *something*. Maybe we can somehow find out what it is!"

Next morning in the playground at break-time, we broke away from the kick-about and found Graeme squatting in the roots of a tree, carving letters into a piece of wood with a pen-knife. I asked him, "Hi, Twiggy, what are you up to there?"

"W-w-w-what d-d-d-does it look like, H-H-Hallam?" he answered back brusquely, "I'm c-c-c-carving my name, of c-c-c-course. G-R-A-E ..."

"Yes, we know how to spell your name, Twiggy," snapped back Sam impatiently, "but what's it *for*?"

"B-b-b-because one day I am going to be a p-p-p-printer like C-C-C-Caxton. Look!" He handed us his piece of wood to look at. It was only then that we realised that he had not cut the letters *inwards*, but *outwards* in relief.

Sam was fascinated. "Look at that, Mark! But how can we print out your name, Twiggy?"

"W-W-W-What w-w-we need," replied Graeme knowledgeably, "is some soot in w-w-wax. Or some b-b-b-boot-p-p-p-polish even ..."

The upshot of this rather protracted discussion was that, after a few run-ins with Matron because of the state of our hands, the three of us got the School Printing Club started, with Twiggy in charge. Soon he was getting little jobs to print. First, he did business cards for me and Sam; then everybody wanted them, and suddenly Twiggy found himself the centre of unaccustomed attention. Finally, Mr Leaming, the Music Master, asked him if he could print the school concert programme, and this was achieved with great skill and pride by our Club. (Incidentally, I saw in a recent Old Boys Newsletter, that the school send round annually, that *Graeme Lithos* has now hit the big time ...)

And so we all grew up.

I first became aware of myself (sexually, that is) shortly before my eleventh birthday.

Matron had drawn me on one side after games one afternoon and told me that no more was I to shower with the other boys, but should, instead, in the future, use the bath next to my dormitory. While I was aware that this was a senior boys' privilege, I had, initially, no inkling as to its technical significance – until Sam had suddenly burst into my bathroom late one afternoon, and had stopped aghast as he had beheld my private parts. Gasping in affected awe, he declared with great authority: "Crikey, Mark, it's just monstrous already – and it's not even stiff, for heaven's sake. Wow! You're sure you're not turning into a freak? From now on I am going to call you Marcus Maximus." And he had skipped away, no doubt to enlighten anyone else who might have even a marginal interest in such matters.

I had whacked a flannel down over the offending area until he had gone, but had then taken a closer look. The equipment *was* bigger, even thinking about it seemed to arouse it, and, most interesting of all, there was just the suggestion of black follicles beginning to show around the base. Both my parents are dark-haired, and I am now a 'blue-beard' who usually shaves night and morning; so I was exceedingly mature for my age.

Sam, on the other hand, was slight, blonde, blue-eyed and way behind me in this department, to his obvious frustration – although, as it turned out, he made up for it by his superior breadth of medical knowledge in such crucial matters.

Then one day, in our final year, disaster struck.

I was called to the headmaster's drawing-room to be faced with shocking news: Sam's father was dying. No, not an accident in one of his cars; the irony was that he had suddenly been diagnosed, far too late, with lung cancer. "You are Sam's closest friend, aren't you, Mark?" the headmaster asked. "Sam has requested that you should go with him when his mother comes down to collect him tomorrow. Do you think you can handle this?" I nodded. "Good, I am sure you can, boy."

It was a five hour drive over to Paradise Park, the Nielsen homestead in Suffolk. Their housekeeper, Mrs Bardsley, greeted us at the door. Sam gave her a hug, and I shook her hand warmly.

"You all three go on up and see the master!" she said. "I'll have a cooked tea ready for you boys in half an hour." We went up the old oak staircase and were met by a nurse who was administering regular morphine injections to Sam's father.

I had only properly met him once before when he had come over for one of our Sunday lunch outings, but had seen him at quite a few school events. He was barely thirty-four, but now looked sixty. He had Sam's piercing blue eyes. "Thanks for coming, Mark; you are a wonderful friend." His breathing was strained, and obviously coughing was very painful. "Promise me something, will you?"

I nodded cautiously, and sat down beside him on the bed, while Mrs Nielsen adjusted his pillows.

He took my hand and his eyes bored into me, even as Sam's had done on that day nearly three years earlier when our friendship had first begun. "Two things, actually, old chap: I want you to help Helen look after Sam, will you, because she is now going to have a business to run. And I want it to be an even *more* brilliant business when Sam's old enough to take over."

Held still by these bright, penetrating eyes socketed into the wasted body, I promised.

"Oh, and the other thing: never let my son touch a ciga-rette, *ever*! OK? Sure? Helen kept warning me, but I could never manage without that blessed weed." He seemed relieved and relaxed after this interchange. We all sat round his bed saying very little. After half an hour, he started to become increasingly distressed, and soon the nurse came back to give him another injection.

We went downstairs for the meal that Mrs Bardsley had cooked for us. It was a real country meal, but we could eat very little of it, and there still seemed not much to say.

When we went upstairs again to say our goodbyes, Sam's father was asleep ... or very groggy. Sam knelt beside him and gave him a huge hug. After a while, as he got up, I could see that both were crying, and I marvelled at their tight relationship – so different from that between me and my own father.

On the journey down Sam had sat next to his mother in the front of the *Saab*, but, on our way back to the school, he joined me in the back and held my hand in an almost vice-like grip, as he stared unseeing at the road ahead. I looked at him a couple of times, and the pain in his eyes was palpable.

Not many mornings later Sam was not at breakfast: his mother had collected him again, this time in the middle of the night. At Assembly the headmaster made an announcement, which made such an impression upon me that I can hear him speaking even now: "Boys, a very terrible thing happened in the early hours of this morning: one of our Old Boys died. Mr Peter Nielsen, Sam's father, whom we have often seen here at the school, passed away. What is so particularly awful about this news is that he was only aged thirty-four, a lot younger than many of those who teach you here. As the Bible says: 'We know neither the day, nor the hour ...' He did not die suddenly; he died slowly, bravely and painfully over a period of some three months.

"Mr Nielsen was a very wonderful and generous man, particularly towards his old school. He packed a very great deal into a short and hectic life in the world of motor-racing, and, if he were destined to die prematurely, we might have expected that to have happened in one of his racing cars; but he was too brilliant and professional a driver for that. But motor-racing is, like many jobs in life, very, very stressful: and, once he had started smoking, he was never able to give up. And it was this heavy smoking that gave him the lung cancer that destroyed him. A terrible loss, therefore, to each and everyone of us. Our loss is Heaven's gain. I hope that each one of you will manage to achieve as much as he did in this life that is God's gift to you ... and learn the lesson of his most premature death.

"So, let us now think of and pray for Sam, Mrs Nielsen, and Mr Nielsen's parents!"

Then Pillar, the head boy, recited a special poem, which was always done when something terrible had happened to someone in the school, after which I had to sing the last verse of "Abide With Me" – which, in the circumstances, I found as difficult as Pillar had done.

Finally, the headmaster asked us all to try not to cry any more and to sing "Who Would True Valour See" as loudly as we possibly could. We then all went to our classrooms, nobody making a sound. It was an awesome day for us youngsters.

I was called out of lessons a few days later to join a group in the headmaster's drawing room. As I stood next to Sam rather awkwardly, he whispered in my ear: "Mark, I want you to give my Mamma a hug: you *must* make her *cry*."

Supported by another woman, who was clearly her sister, Mrs Nielsen was standing like a statue, not hearing a word that anyone said. At first I hesitated, but finally I walked across and embraced her – I was nearly as tall as she was by now, and her scent in my nostrils was just wonderful – and almost immediately her restraint melted. Bit by bit she began to cry, and I offered her my not very clean handkerchief, which she accepted gratefully. After a while her shaking eased: "Oh, you are such a thoughtful boy, Mark. But, you know, it's Sam you should be hugging, not me ..."

"Oh, he'll be all right with us," I replied with mock cheerfulness. And Sam, who was standing behind her, nodded vigorously. And so he was, or seemed to be. Everybody liked Sam anyway, and he seemed either to have got over his father's death very quickly – or it had yet to sink in.

The headmaster had appointed me to represent the school at the funeral and had given me a huge wreath in the middle of which was attached a special card that Twiggy's Printing

Club had created. I had special instructions to give it to the funeral director to be placed with all the other wreaths.

So we set off for Suffolk once more, Mrs Nielsen's sister driving, and spent that night at Paradise Park.

The funeral next day was not a very inspiring affair, and I do not remember a great deal about it except Sam walking with his mother in front of the coffin to *Siegfried's Funeral March*. Both he and I agreed afterwards that the singing was rather 'pathetic' and wished we had thought to take a hand in brightening up the service with some livelier hymns.

Mrs Nielsen seemed to be steadier and more at peace when she dropped us both back at the school, if emotionally and physically drained. As I gave her a long hug and a kiss, and breathed in her fragrance once more, I noticed, really for the first time, what an intensely beautiful woman she was.

That night I had only been asleep for about an hour, when Matron woke me up and asked me to come with her. She took me to the sickroom where Sam was lying weeping as if his heart would break. "Would you stay with him, Mark?" She lifted the sheet and blanket at the side of the bed, but I looked at her questioningly. After a second's hesitation she nodded: "He needs a cuddle, the poor wee lad; I think I can trust you not to misbehave ..." I took off my dressing-gown, and slipped into the bed beside him. Clearly she too was not entirely happy with this solution, but she felt I was the only answer. Sam immediately snuggled up with his face buried in my side.

After a while his weeping ebbed away and soon he was sound asleep. For a while I felt like a father comforting his son; I was so desperately sorry for my friend – but also rather proud of my new role. Once Sam was firmly asleep and had turned away, I slipped back to my own bed.

Next day, though, he brought me back to earth with one of his cackier comments: "Thanks for bedding down with me last night, big boy, but better not make a habit of it, eh? We don't want the servants talking. And anyway you're a bit too big for me, remember?" He smirked knowingly, and danced away before I could take a swipe at him. At least he seemed to be back to his old self.

Youngsters are very resilient, and our lives quickly returned to their former rhythm.

Academically I was headed for a scholarship, and rugger was my sport. I made Head Boy, and ensured that we won most of our rugby fixtures. I was also Head Chorister with Sam as Underhead. My voice had fully broken by the time I left, so I was probably the only leaver in the school's history to be singing baritone at the school concert.

As the climax of the concert, Mr Leaming secretly coached Sam and me to sing Rachmaninov's *Ave Maria* (Op. 37, No. 6). This is not a greatly known anthem, but it is a most beautiful, haunting work, quite short, easy to sing quite well with no very high treble notes, but very hard to sing *really* well. Mr Leaming came up with a version that drew on the best of the upper and lower lines, and we had to learn it by heart. In retrospect, this was all quite a tall order, but, as kids, we knew no better, we just got on with it. Sam was the star, I was his bass backing. Our performance brought the house down, everyone cheered and stamped, and all the mothers wept, while the fathers pretended not to.

It was a memorable note on which to end some very happy days.

I had won my scholarship, but was even more delighted to discover that Sam had scraped into the same school on his Common Entrance results. He gave me his usual impish, semi-mournful smile: "I am relying on you, Mark, to help me stay there. It's going to be just *marvellous* if I immediately go and fail my first term's exams, and get the push."

To me it was vital we maintain our friendship: not only did I want to go on seeing Sam, but his mother had become more and more important to me in a way that I could not yet define. With me in College House and him in one of the town houses, keeping in touch was not going to be so easy.

My great game remained Rugby Football, and I prided myself on the power of my kicks out of defence; soon I was in the top team in my year. I also decided to take up rowing in the summer. Sam on the other hand was the artist and the engineer: he spent much of his spare time either painting water-colours in the Drawing Department, playing flute in the Music Department or down in the Mech School turning things on lathes. He was also an accomplished swimmer, creating ever more complex dives off the top-board, somewhat to the consternation of the swimming instructor. The only other exercise he seemed to take was running with the beagles.

Being already far more mature than my peers, sex, though a constant topic for discussion amongst other team members and friends, did not figure high on my agenda. In my last two years at prep school I had accepted wet dreams as an almost tiresome routine, accompanied usually by the fantasy visions of blonde girls with well-formed breasts and bottoms; but these damp episodes were little more than a frustrating inconvenience. Masturbation had not been a topic of conversation at Prep. For new boys at public school, on the other hand, this seemed to be a predominating, fascinating subject, presumably for the mutual reassurance adolescents seek as they explore their new-found sexuality, both separately and, in a few cases, together. But I found it all rather childish and never felt the same overwhelming need to indulge. Somehow I was always too busy – or too exhausted.

But Sam and I were determined to maintain our ritual Sunday lunches. Because the school was a lot closer to Sam's home, Mrs Nielsen would take us out on alternate Sundays, and I expect she was lonely as well. We would sing together in the choir at morning chapel, and she would always be there in one of the parents' stalls. Then, as before, we would go out and explore a different lunch venue each time, following this up with skating, water-slides or a visit to the zoo. (We soon stopped going to the zoo because Sam said 'he hated seeing animals caged up so'.)

One Sunday she told us over lunch that we were going to

spend that afternoon picking up a dog. I was not particularly interested by this idea, as I was not much into dogs, but Sam was thrilled. "What breed, Mamma?"

"I've decided on a greyhound. My parents had one long ago. I do get a bit lonely on my own now, you see, and he will guard me, make me take exercise and generally keep me company."

"Sounds wonderful," said Sam. "I'm really excited."

After lunch we drove the twenty miles to a large, private house near Bracknell. As we got out of the *Volvo*, our gaze was at once caught by a row of pointed snouts staring at us excitedly – but silently – through the long drawing-room window. Then the owners opened the front-door, and out poured nine silken-haired greyhounds of various genders and hues; individually they began silently checking us over.

"Come in, the Nielsens!" said the lady of the house quietly. "We've all been expecting you."

We all sat ourselves down in this vast room with greyhounds stretched out over various areas of the floor, while the eldest climbed stiffly onto his own special rug-covered sofa, and stretched out. Sam was clearly captivated.

Tea was brought, and general conversation ensued, as the dog rescue people carefully checked with Mrs Nielsen all that had obviously been previously discussed by phone and correspondence. After a while Sam could not control himself any longer: "But which one is ours?"

Mr Farthing smiled, "All right, you're on. Flash, introduce yourself!" One of the faun-coloured animals got up at once, walked across to Sam, laid his muzzle on Sam's knee, and stared up at him.

"Oh, you absolute darling!" said Sam ecstatically, at which the dog raised one paw as a signal, then launched both front paws onto Sam's shoulders, licked his face, then got down again. He then came over to me, a little uncertainly. I patted his head with equal uncertainty. Then he went over to Mrs Nielsen, laid his muzzle on her knee and stared up at her.

"Oh, Flash! Can you *really* look after me, do you think?" The dog reached slowly up, and gently licked her face. And then I noticed that tears were running down her cheek – and I suddenly realised what a desperately lonely person she was. And I wanted to hug her.

Sam and I were fascinated. "But how does he *know*?" I asked.

Mr Farthing was about to reply, but Mrs Nielsen raised her hand: "Obviously they have no capacity to speak, but they *listen* to every ounce of conversation, ready instantly to pick up on key-phrases that they go on learning by rote."

"Absolutely right," Mr Farthing followed on. "All dogs interact with humans this way, but greyhounds are particularly acute at it. Now listen and watch! I am going to go on talking, and then I'll slip in a key-phrase. This morning Sonia and I went to Church, our vicar has a bee in his bonnet about the King James Bible – dogs for a walk – and insists ..." His tone of voice had not altered, but every animal had immediately risen as one, all eyes fixed on the speaker. He then smiled and shook his head: "No-o-o-o-o!" They all lay down again in unison, and the elderly resident, who was still half way through levering himself off the sofa, recomposed himself with a slow, irritated grunt.

"Well, clearly that's all right then," said Mrs Farthing, with obvious relief. "Be warned, he is called Flash, not just because he is quick, but because he can be quick with any left-overs round the kitchen if they are not put away."

Once tea was over, Flash's personal accoutrements were laid out carefully in the back of the estate car; then Mrs Nielsen invited him to climb aboard. He sniffed everything carefully, then climbed up and sat up there expectantly, as the door was gently closed behind him. And so we set off back to the school.

Thus it was that Flash joined our little team. Later, as the time passed, I came to understand that he embodied all that is best in a dog. He never barked unless threatened by another dog. Although he was not a particularly good guard-dog – he was easily scared and hated loud noises, like gun-shots, loud music or family rows – he was immensely peaceable and friendly. He never forgot a face, or rather, a smell.

Once I had passed muster, whenever we met, he would wait for the other greetings to be complete, then he would wander up quietly, look at me with his mournful brown eyes, then either nuzzle me gently or hop up on his hind-legs, stretching his long, lean body up to put his front paws onto my shoulders and give me a lick, as if to say, "Yes, it's me, as well; good to see you around, old friend!" His ethos was love, loyalty and reliability, the fundamentals of any true friendship – or marriage, for that matter. He insisted on being involved in absolutely everything his mistress did, however mundane; to be left behind at home was the ultimate rebuff.

Apart from his restricted diet, his most favourite treat was to be taken down in the car to the works test-track when the factory was closed. Mrs Nielsen would let him out and then drive slowly round the track with him loping along behind. Once he was settled into a comfortable stride and breathing steadily, she would suddenly accelerate up to 40 mph, letting him stretch his lungs for a few hundred yards, then slow down again for a while to let him recover, then stop and let him lap at the drink that she had brought along with her.

It was towards the end of that first summer term that practical sex suddenly popped up between Sam and me. We were out walking down by the river one Sunday evening, after his mother had dropped us off, when he suddenly stopped, leant against a tree, looked at me and said, out of the blue, "Have you started wanking yet?" Pretending I was not the slightest bit taken aback, I said, "No, not really bothered much about it actually ..."

"Oh, you *should*," he insisted, "I had a go the first time about three weeks ago, and it's an absolutely fantastic feeling underneath; I saved up a bit and did it twice on the trot the other night. There's another chap in my house, Bolsover Minor, who says he's managed it five times in twenty-four hours ... but I don't think I believe him 'cause he would have had a heart attack during lessons. Yes, he said he even did it once during Divinity ...! Imagine what God must have thought!" Sam was full of it. "You should really have a go, you know: I'll show you if you like ..." he went on, only slightly coyly. His hands were deep in his pockets and he was massaging an obvious erection.

I instinctively declined the offer, and he was clearly deeply disappointed when one so dim as he – as he saw himself – had something so very special to show off to one so clever as me. In compensation, when we reached his room, I accepted his offer of a large folded glossy piece of paper from a magazine from his top cupboard, which – at great personal sacrifice – he would let me borrow. It would help me in my quest, he assured me. "Better keep it! Don't want it back all covered in your dried spunk, mate." That night, after lights out, I duly unfolded the piece of paper on my pillow and viewed it with a torch. It had been taken from a sex magazine. This girl was lying on her back completely naked with her knees drawn up and parted with the soles of her feet pressed together. The sight gave me an immediate erection, and at once I found myself thinking of Sam's mother, of all people. I turned off the torch, pulled my pants off and lay face down fondling my parts, smiling as I fell asleep with this visionary lady in my mind spread out beneath me. An hour later I emerged from the most erotic dream slithering in the after-effects of the most effervescent wet-dream ever. As I dried the sheet off with a towel I devoutly wished my dream could become a reality.

A couple of days before the end of term Sam begged me to come out with him on a Beagle Run. I was not rowing that afternoon and was at a loose end; so, unsuspecting, I agreed. After a while he broke away from the pack and led us off into some trees. He suddenly stopped, leant back against a tree in his familiar, arrogant pose, eyes a-twinkle with his hands cradling his usual erection, gave me that impish look of his and asked, "Did you do it? Did you wank off?" As he said it, I caught the resemblance between him and his mother, and in a way that I found difficult to explain, he excited me.

"Not really," I replied a bit breathless – from the running, of course. "But that picture you gave me got me shooting everywhere in my sleep ..."

"No, that's no good." He sounded frustrated. "Look, watch!" Before I could think, he had zipped down the front of his white beagling trousers and dragged them down to his knees. Then down came his skimpy, golden silk underpants as well. And there he was with his erection standing up from a cluster of white hairs like a little snake with a glistening one-eyed head – not quite as big as mine by then, I may say – staring up at me. I could see his balls in his scrotum were up as tight as a drum and his foreskin was back ready for action. He started rubbing: "Go on, you do it!" I hesitated. He took my hand and placed it round his penis. I stroked a little tentatively. "No, come on!" he breathed. He spun round, placing his bare bottom, bare anyway but for his shirt-tails, against my front and took my hand again. This was easier, less awkward. Then he got me to touch his balls with my other hand. I increased the motion in accordance with his excited directions, breathing in the musky smell of his neck. In a few moments I felt his back spasm and he let out a gasp: "Gawd, that was great, Mark, I almost reached the other tree!" He turned to me with a great grin on his face. "Now you, your turn!" He dodged round behind me, put his hand against my belly. I felt I should be fending him off, but just at that moment I did not want to. After some preliminary caressing through the top of my pants, he slipped his hand down into my underpants. Then I unbuttoned my trousers and suddenly I was standing as naked as he was, trousers and pants round my ankles. But this time I could feel his privates against my bare bottom. I suddenly feared what he might do: "No, Sam, not that!" But I need not have worried. He rubbed me away with amazing skill, a pressure started to build in my lower bottom and suddenly I was arching my back in response to the exquisite sensation of the pent-up sperm shooting across the glen.

My first wank, and it had not even been I who had made it happen ... Sam moved round to face me and whispered in triumph, "Wasn't that something, Mark? ... At last!" Glancing round, just to make absolutely sure no one had spotted our pranks, we pulled up our things and started walking back to the school saying nothing, both sharing an awkward, slightly guilty – yet exultant – feeling. We stopped outside the entrance to College House. He turned and looked at me rather solemnly, "Not a word to a soul, will you? Our secret."

"Hardly!" I protested. "Mind you, I am not going to make a habit of it either."

He smiled knowingly and skipped off, as ever, like a fawn. For quite some while afterwards I just sat in my cubicle thinking about the whole episode. Granted Sam was what some had already called 'really quite a pretty little chap', and no doubt he was having to turn away the nightly attentions of a whole host of randy 5th formers, but I had no discernible homosexual feelings towards him, though I suspected, even feared, he probably had some for me. In hindsight I suppose he saw me more as the dominant male in a male/female relationship. Certainly he is no homosexual now: last time I saw him he appeared to be having quite a steady relationship with an utterly gorgeous Phillipino girl ...

During the summer holidays I located another girlie magazine with the usual array of ladies displaying all their most exciting parts. I would try to let the pressure in my loins really build up over a number of days and nights. Then, on a pre-ordained night, I would, in my imaginings, invite a particular lady around to my lair, and then fantasize a full love-making act with as little rubbing as possible. It became something of a challenge, and I would get furious with my body if this fine record of abstinence was broken by a wet dream, and I would have to start all over again.

But quite soon I stopped wasting my money on these publications, as, more and more, the vision of Sam's mother featured in my imaginings. Whenever we met for our lunches she seemed to find it quite natural that we should embrace, and I would be overwhelmed by her fragrance – and the bulges of her exquisite breasts beneath her dress. I suppose all growing boys love to fantasize. For me she became one of the

Greek goddesses featured in a photograph on a vase in my 'Iliad' Greek text-book. I had learnt long ago that Sam's mother was called Helen; for me she was simply Helen of Troy.

Such guilty thoughts never really bothered me in themselves. And, of course, I never breathed a word about them to Sam, nor made the slightest overt indication of my secret affection for his mother. But sometimes I dreaded he might one day guess. Worse still I feared that one day *she* might guess. And I had to be very careful not to let slip even an inkling of these feelings at our fortnightly lunches.

At home in the holidays at the RAF station in Germany I would tell my parents how wonderful the Nielsens were, and what a wonderful mother I thought Mrs Nielsen was. This was, maybe, somewhat thoughtless in the light of subsequent events, because I think they began rather to resent her and my apparent fascination for her. But, on my side, I was aware that, although they very occasionally came over to England to visit my younger sister in Kent, they had never driven further across the country to visit *me*. I suppose their argument was that I was a fit, healthy and intelligent lad with a well-developed mask of self-assurance, and that I should be allowed to learn about life without persistent interference from them. Whereas my sister, on the other hand, was quite a bit younger, and, well, she was a girl, after all.

Yet it never crossed my mind at the time that my father and mother should be beginning to harbour suspicions as to my true feelings for Sam's mother.

Chapter 2

Elopement

A year passed. Sam and I were both going to be fifteen in just a few months.

I was still into rugby and rowing. Sam was a swimmer and had now added sculpture to his water-colouring; he was also lead flautist in the school orchestra. I rather missed our former close company, but our interests just did not coincide. Although we visited each other in our rooms occasionally, and I would not have missed our twice-termly Sunday lunches in any circumstances, our only regular point of contact was the School Choir. At these Sunday lunches Sam always plied his mother with questions about their racing business. He was already spending all his holidays down at the works or at race-meetings, while Mrs Nielsen continued to handle all the money side. I was for ever impressed by her quiet grasp of the whole motor-racing scene, and at the same time by her amazing serenity – and, increasingly, by her beauty and by her desirability.

It is very difficult, after thirty years, really to trace the stages of my falling in love with Helen. I think at that moment, like most adolescents, I was fantasizing by day and by night, and night after night, what 'it' would be like: would it really feel as utterly magical as we all believed it should, when finally 'it' happened? As my growing up rocketed ahead, she, and she alone, seemed to encompass all that I sought: she was a kind and generous mother, she still had a superb figure, her skin was silken, her scent captivating. Although not Nordic herself, she had the same Norse maritime, good looks that her Swedish husband had loved and cherished. Maybe it *was* only lust; but I believed, as only a fourteen year old can, that I loved her more than any woman in the world. All I wanted was to curl up in her embrace, kiss her heavenly lips and body – and relieve the agonising ache in my loins that eternally tormented me. And yet she was, of course, totally unattainable.

One Sunday afternoon, at Sam's urgings, Mrs Nielsen drove us down to a little indoor Go-Kart track in Guildford that he had heard about. The moment we entered the place, Sam was transformed. He dressed me and his mother up in some basic protective gear, selected three carts with an expert eye, got the two of us started, then raced away. She and I pottered unsteadily along like novices while Sam tore round at a relentless pace, never stopping, never faltering, never drawing breath. Soon the manager had to approach her for more money: we disembarked, and stood side by side admiring Sam's amazing skill at the wheel of his car. I took his mother's hand; she did not withdraw it. Then we sat down together, not saying very much but enjoying each other's presence.

After an hour the manager made Sam stop, and, recognising a 'natural', led him proudly to a different car which was hidden away in a corner. It was longer, sleeker, faster. Sam had the measure of it in a couple of circuits; then on and on he raced till finally Mrs Nielsen ran out of cash and she and the manager agreed a final cheque. After nearly three hours at the wheel Sam was finally persuaded to relent. As we waited for him to get changed, the manager said to Mrs Nielsen: "That boy is by far and away the most skilful driver I have *ever* seen on my track. Properly trained, he could have a bright future, you know."

Sam's mother smiled quietly, "Yes, I hope he will."

Over the years I had become increasingly aware of the contrast between the Nielsen home and family life and that of my own. I loved – no, respected – my parents; I had been brought up to uphold their austere standards, but, while I was cognisant of the financial sacrifices they had made to put my sister and me through private education, yet I could never escape the sub-conscious feeling that, if only in part, they had opted out of my later upbringing because they simply believed that the private school regime would do the job of raising me to responsible citizenship far more adequately than they could. Our home was on an active RAF station on the Dutch-German border, my father was a Wing Commander, whom I hardly ever saw, and my mother was determined that I should not be spoiled. The effective outcome seemed to be that my younger sister got spoiled instead. The further consequence, in the longer term, was that I saw as little of them and as much of Sam, and of his mother, as I could.

One Sunday evening late that second summer term, after Mrs Nielsen (and Flash) had taken the two of us out to one of our lunches, Sam accompanied me round to my room in College House to talk about 'something important'. We had never mentioned again the incident in the woods when he had initiated me. Nonetheless, I was somewhat apprehensive until, having sat down and stared out at the river for a while, he turned, looked me in the eye, gave me one of his winning smiles, and then blurted out: "These hols, what are you lot doing this summer, Marcus?"

"Not much, so far as I know. Austria maybe," I replied uncertainly.

"Well, how about you coming down to the sea-side with my mamma, Flash and me for a week or two? We could all four of us have such a *great* time." He looked at me almost pleading.

The prospect genuinely delighted me – for a thousand reasons. "Sounds a super idea! When do we go? Where do we go? Just let me know how much dosh we should chip in!"

Sam looked excited and relieved. "Well, my mamma suggested to me the last fortnight of the summer holidays. I am not sure where, but maybe Bournemouth or somewhere. Nice beaches …"

"Who's idea is this?" I questioned, genuinely curious, "Yours or your mother's?"

"Both, of course!" he replied without a moment's hesitation.

So I wrote to my mother. Curiously, she had never met Helen Nielsen but, having written to her once or twice a long time ago to thank her for taking me out, my parents had accepted that any long-term friend of mine must be an acceptable influence, without ever bothering to find out more or even ring her.

My mother wrote back to say that the only thing that had already been arranged on our side was that she, my sister and I were to go walking up mountains in the Austrian Alps. My father would be coming down just for the first four days, then be flying back to Bruggen. I had always loved Austria, but I decided that I could, this time, have chosen more thrilling company. So it was arranged. The term finished. Austria happened.

To be fair, it was – or would have been, but for my secret yearnings – a wonderful trip. My parents had booked us into a lovely hotel overlooking a lake to the east of Salzburg. It was phenomenally hot. By day we bathed in, rowed or sailed on the lake or climbed the mountains that surrounded us; we ate and we slept. By night, when it was cooler, we went into Salzburg to enjoy Mozart at the Felsenreitschule, 'Jedermann', the Puppets, and see all the 'Sound of Music' locations. It was by any standards a great fortnight – had I not been so distrait, and my nights so tormented. I feared that my longing to get back to England and the Nielsens might not have been well enough concealed.

On our return to Bruggen, my father took time off and gave me a couple of driving lessons in a corner of the air-field, and that was really our only point of contact. Oh, except when, one evening after supper, he took me on one side in his study, and gave me a 'Daddy Talk'. I listened patiently while he ploughed on through a minefield of circumlocutions; I nodded at appropriate intervals. His concluding words were: "Normally, son, I would not have raised this tricky subject so early (early!), but you have always been very advanced for your age; these urges will soon (soon!) start coming upon you; naturally I am anxious that you should not go astray and let the side down by some indiscretion – I am sure you never would do that, of course, not on purpose, that is. But fore-warned is forearmed. Temptations present themselves to all of us in many forms. Maybe you have even been tempted already?"

I declined to comment, but thanked him for his thorough-ness and openness, which, I said, was backed up by all the situations that daily (and nightly) did indeed present them-selves at school ...

No more was said on the subject, and I was left with the feeling that my father believed he had done his paternal duty towards his son, as well as giving me an overdue warning. But I, for my part, was *not* going to be frustrated in my secret mission.

At long last I was on the plane back to Luton, and Sam and his mother were duly there to pick me up. Mrs Nielsen and I embraced with such warmth that Sam finally had to say, "Oh, come on you two!" rather petulantly, and I realised at once that I should be a little more guarded in my demonstrations of affection.

We went straight to our cinema at Haverhill to take in some film or other, bought fish-and-chips, got home late, and went more or less straight to bed. As I lay there, I felt I had come home.

I was about to turn out my light when there was a knock on my door, and Sam's mother looked in to see if I needed anything. Then she sat down on the bed, took my hand and gazed at me. She had Sam's hair, eyes and beautiful fingers. I was instantly aroused. "Thank you for coming, Mark!" she said quietly. "We had been so hoping you would. Now that you are so much one of our family, will you do something for me?" She got up, as I nodded. "I want you to start calling me Helen? Do you mind?" I nodded again, and turned out the light as she left.

Contrarily, this visit left me feeling how unattainable my goal really was: it was utterly absurd to think that we could ever be together. Granted she was nearly eighteen years older than I, but, physically, spiritually, she was the female replica of her son! She was also organised, generous, fun-loving and serene, in all a wonderful mother. She was simply possessed of so many of those qualities that I so missed in my own austere parents. But she was Sam's mother, *not* my lover. She never could be.

But, as before, I imagined myself snuggled up in the loving embrace of *the* most beautiful woman. And, as before on so many other nights, I was duly wakened after some hours by the inevitable consequences of my hectic dreaming.

We packed up the *Volvo* Estate and set off early for the Dorset coast, I in the front with Helen, Sam in the back with Flash across his lap. To pass the time, Helen asked us general knowledge questions from her encyclopaedic brain, and then Sam and I sang her pieces from our choral repertoire.

At one stage I asked vaguely, "So, where are we staying in Bournemouth, then?"

"Actually," said Helen, "we're not quite going to Bournemouth; we've been invited to stay with an old friend of Peter's at Studland, west round the coast a bit from Bournemouth. He's got rather a nice house there. Cavalry officer, family owns a brewery, he and his wife have just been through a rather messy divorce ..."

This news should have set the alarm-bells ringing in my brain, but they did not: I was too innocent.

Having stopped at a pub for lunch, we arrived at this rambling 16th century thatched-roof cottage. There was nobody there except for a horse that gazed at us curiously over an adjacent gate. "Oh, look," said Sam, adoringly, "a pure-bred Arab stallion!" They are shy, difficult creatures, but after a very few minutes, the horse, Sam and Flash were best mates.

Helen found the key and we went in and explored. "Gervaise said he should be back from Lulworth at about 5:30. As it's so nice, shall we go down on the beach?" Following some written instructions, she found our rooms: she had one room, Sam and I had another with separate beds next door. We dumped our suitcases and got out our swimsuits and towels. Helen added to the original note, and all four of us headed down to the beach on foot, as it was only about half a mile away.

The air was oppressively hot. Sam, was first in. "*Bloody hell!* It's *freezing*. This'll really shrink those monstrous assets of yours, Marcus," he shouted.

"Sam!" came Helen's reprimand. "Our guest can do without those sort of comments, please."

I had hardly even heard Sam's remark, breathless as I was at the beauty of Helen in her bathing-suit.

"Well, be warned, Mamma, he looks like an elephant under the shower, I can tell you."

"Sam, that's *enough*."

This interchange drove me straight into the sea to kill my erection before either of the other two could notice it. I headed straight for Sam, picked him up in simulated rage, held him high above my head like a surf-board, then hurled him out to sea. I had caught him off-guard, so, good swimmer that he was, he came up spluttering: "You total bastard!"

"Serves you right," called Helen in unconditional approval.

Knowing he was no match for me, Sam resorted to splashing his mother who was gingerly wading in.

"Sam Nielsen! You will be sent to bed *without* a sweet *or* your story," Helen chided him.

In the meantime Flash was guarding our clothes from higher up the beach, watching our antics with disdain. Despite Sam's entreaties, nothing would persuade him down to the water, an element which he loathed. Finally Sam lifted him round his shoulders, carried him into deep water, then lowered the quaking beast into the sea for his first swim. Flash struck out back to the beach, got out, shook himself a couple of times in evident disgust, and returned to his post, taking a mild revenge by rolling damply on Sam's clothes.

After our swim we lay together basking in the heat. I thought, "This is the most wonderful fun."

After an hour we were starting to get chilly, and decided to head back to the house. Half way home, we were met by our host on the stallion, trumpeting a horn. He was still in uniform with khaki forage-cap and service-dress and bright purple trousers. He jumped down, embraced Helen warmly, then shook us each by the hand. "Gervaise Lockhart."

"Captain the Honourable," added Helen.

He chuckled. "I think will dispense with handles. Just call me 'Sir' – like the men. No, Gervaise'll do." He sized us up. "So, you're Mark? I remember you Sam, when you were a *really* little lad. Fancy a ride?"

Sam nodded without hesitation, and accepted a lift up. He rode this tricky animal like a master, and immediately drew admiring comments on his horsemanship from its owner, "Do you ride a lot?"

Sam shook his head: "Never ridden a horse in my life."

"Amazing!" Lockhart was obviously genuinely impressed.

Seeing him and Helen in animated conversation together, my hopes ebbed away. Initially, anyway, I quite liked this cavalry officer, notwithstanding the fact that he was detaching the object of my affections from before my very eyes.

Once we got back into the house, he poured Helen and himself stiff drinks, and pulled us some coke bottles out of the fridge. "Just help yourselves any time, boys! Now, what do we want for supper?" He produced a menu-card off the kitchen shelf. "Just order what you like, Indian, Chinese, English! Go for it! And I'll phone the order through for the nosh-wallah to bring it up from Swanage. Frankly, my cooking's not up to much."

After some discussion we all went for a massive Chinese array, which he duly ordered. "Right, it'll be delivered in an hour: that'll give us just time to change for dinner and have another drink. I say 'change': by that I mean, lads, at least put on a tie – to keep up appearances."

That dinner proved quite a revelation, as I studied my rival. Bit by bit I learnt his father was a viscount, that he was in charge of Guided Weapons training at the local Army camp – and that he was very attentive towards Helen. She, I was glad to note, did not seem to be seriously returning his attentions – and my hopes rose a little. He was also well educated in the classics; indeed he had been to the same public school as Sam and I.

As supper progressed, he talked endlessly about every topic under the sun – mostly about the Cold War and the flawed (as he saw it) policy of Nuclear Deterrence. Sam and I tried to keep up, but he showed little interest in what we had to contribute. We noticed that he seemed to be drinking huge amounts of wine, port and liqueurs, and was then becoming increasingly peeved that Helen was not matching his rate of consumption. Finally he lit up a foul-smelling cigarillo, which I could not abide.

Quietly I said I was feeling tired, thanked our host, kissed Helen 'Goodnight' and went to bed. Sam followed up not long after.

It was becoming increasingly hot and sticky, and we lay on our beds with nothing on, talking about our host.

"My," said Sam. "That was quite a feed. But I don't know for how long I'll be able to stomach the man Lockhart: he is so *arrogant*. Poor Mamma!"

"Yes! He is, isn't he? And that vile cheroot. God, it's hot. Difficult to go to sleep."

"Well, I'm going to have the father-and-mother of a wank – sovereign remedy for sleeplessness. You wouldn't care to do the honours, would you?" He jiggled his erection at me in the fading light.

"No, Sam. You can do your own dirty work, thank you."

"Spoil-sport! I can see *you* have got a stiffy on; or is it always like that?"

I rolled over to hide the offending member. All I could think of, as ever, was Helen. Soon she would be lying there in the next room, all alone, serene, goddess-like … Suddenly I had a ghastly thought: what if she was even now being persuaded into the arms of that vile cavalry officer. Firmly I dismissed the idea. But how could I ever attain her? How could I ever reveal to her my secret longings? – longings that were manifested by the unstoppable ache in my loins. I lay there and lay there, plotting how this might be achieved. What pretext could I devise?

Finally, an age later, as if to reward my importunity, the weather came to my aid at about three o'clock in the morning.

Thunder and lightning: the storm suddenly broke. I checked that Sam was still well asleep – thunderstorms never seemed to bother him – then, feigning terror, I put on my pants and dressing-gown, tip-toed out and straight into Helen's room. "Helen, can I come in with you till this lightning stops?" I whispered in the dark. "Thunderstorms always scare me." "You poor boy! All right, just for a short while then." She lifted the side of the sheet. I took off my dressing-gown; then slid in on the edge of the bed, careful not to touch her. For a while I just lay there scarce able to believe where I was. Then suddenly there was another flash, followed by a huge bang, and I clutched out frantically at her body. It was only as I did so, that I discovered that, in the hot weather, she was absolutely naked, like Sam and I had been. It was the most gorgeous grown-up sensation I had ever, ever experienced. She had instinctively turned towards me, and I just buried my face in her beautifully formed breasts, while my arms embraced her. As the storm raged on, I knew that our fronts were barely an inch apart and I just prayed that I would not give the whole game away by jetting off into my pants.

Sensing something, she said, "I think it might be wiser if I turned over." When she had turned away from me, I moved my hands up gently and cupped her breasts, and she sighed quietly. "Oh, Mark, you are a dear boy. I do love feeling your tickly chest against my back."

For what seemed a lifetime I held her perfect body to me. She could obviously feel my member hard in my pants against the clevis of her bottom. Finally, in desperation, I asked: "Helen, would you mind very much if I took my pants off? They *are* hurting rather ..." She said nothing. I moved away and, with as little fuss as I could, wriggled them off. Suddenly I was erect against her buttocks.

Then she said, "Move down a little bit!" I did so, and she let me slip myself between her legs. And so we were almost truly together, she enclosed inside the hollow of my body. I was in heaven. The world could stand still. I was ready to die. No, I had not entered her, but it was enough. Then suddenly she skilfully touched the end of my penis and moved it up just a little against the warm dampness of her place. And instantly it was all over. With great surges of ecstasy, I jetted my all; torrents of fluid that had been building for days, for years, indeed seemingly for ever, were finally spontaneously pouring forth in this righteous cause.

"Oh Helen, I am so sorry!" was all I could mumble into her ear. I felt victorious, yet mortified. "It's just that I didn't want you getting a baby," I added lamely.

"Don't be sorry, Mark! That often happens the first time. You were absolutely *wonderful*. You were so tender, kindness itself. And don't worry about me: Sam, I am afraid, was the only baby I shall ever have."

We held together for a while longer. It was only now that I became aware that the panting, which I subconsciously thought was our own, was coming *from under the bed*. "Someone's under the bed, Helen," I whispered in horror.

To my surprise she giggled: "Come up, Flash! The thunder's stopped." Very gingerly, the terrified dog wriggled out from his hiding place, stepped daintily up on the bed and settled down between us. "There," said Helen, "is someone whose fear of thunder is genuine – unlike some I know around here ..."

This seemed to be my cue to leave. I made my excuses, "Yes, the thunder *has* stopped, and Sam may wake up." I said, not quite logically.

We kissed; for the first time ever we kissed. I marvelled at her, blessed her, put my underpants and dressing-gown back on, and left her room.

Outside, to my horror, our host was standing by the window, smoking another cheroot, staring out at his stallion. I acknowledged him, and he looked across at me in some curiosity: "Would it be uncharitable to wonder if Eros has been supping at the altar of the beauteous Helen Bountiful?"

I shall never know, even after subsequent events, whether his quite outrageous remark to a fifteen year old was, at the time, meant as a crude jest, or whether he was serious and suspected something. Nevertheless, I froze at his words; then mumbled something about being scared of thunderstorms, and fled back into our room. I lay there quaking, and it was a while before I finally fell asleep.

I awoke to hear Sam and Helen talking quietly in our room. Sam was sitting up on his bed, half dressed. Helen was in the armchair: she had obviously been crying.

"What's up?" I asked, fearing the answer.

Helen made no answer.

"Trouble at t'mill," Sam responded, finally. "Mamma has been having a problem with the excessive attentions of our noble host."

I looked across at Helen.

She finally spoke up, "I think, as I was saying to Sam, we may have to make alternative arrangements. Gervaise has apparently come up with long-term plans for him and for me which I am not entirely happy to fall in with. However he has very kindly organised for you two to spend the morning at the camp. I shall go into Poole and sort out a few things. We'll meet up again at lunch-time."

When we got down to breakfast, Lockhart was reading his paper over a boiled egg. He affected good cheer, and invited us to help ourselves. Once we were settled, he put down his paper. "Right, I am taking you two off to the Tank Museum this morning; hopefully I'll get you a drive in a Scout Car. Do you know what that is?"

"Sort of little tank, isn't it?" replied Sam. "*Rolls-Royce* engine, semi-automatic gear-box?"

"Chip off your dad's old block, I see." He sounded pleased. "Well, eat up, both of you, and let's get going! Wagons roll in twenty minutes; otherwise I'll be late for work."

We squeezed into our host's *Mercedes* open-topped convertible and tore down to Bovington Camp. In the background we could hear the crash of the tanks firing on the Lulworth ranges. He stopped off by some old wooden huts, where we were met by a kindly man immaculately dressed all in black – black overalls, black shiny boots, black beret. He had three chevrons and a crown on his arm and the name Meyrick tailored above his left breast pocket.

"Staff'll see you all right!" said Lockhart. "I'll pick 'em up at the Museum entrance at 1300. OK, Staff? Many thanks!" And drove off at high speed.

As our guide led us into the building, I was immediately aware of an all-pervading smell of boot-polish and engine-oil. The room was full of cut down, see-through models of engines painted in red, black and turquoise. Yet, at the same time, all was spotless.

Sam was immediately captivated. He grabbed at a crank-handle, and watched intently as the pistons moved up and down in response to his rotations. "Wow, what a place, Staff!" For an hour he grilled our guide on every aspect of every engine in the room. And this highly professional man was delighted to oblige such an enthusiast.

The *coup de grâce* was a colossal cut-down gear-box from an old Centurion tank. Sam stared at it in wonderment. "Go on, Staff! Show us how it works, how the gears change!"

"You'd have a seizure if I showed you how to trace the pathways through those epicyclics, Sir ..."

"Try me, Staff!"

I was lost in this maze at a very early stage, but together they traced through all the gears. At the end Sam sat down, gasping, as if he had seen a vision. "Staff, I *must drive that.*"

"Well, I don't know about that really. I'd got a Ferret for you. Mind you, we've still got quite a few Cents that are just operational. But I mean, apart from anything else, with due respect, Sir, you wouldn't even reach the pedals, and ..."

"Even just to sit at the controls, Staff. Please, Staff!"

Phone-calls were made; cups of tea were drunk. Then Meyrick drove us through the camp down to the tank park in his beat-up old left-hand-drive *Volkswagen* Beatle.

I was given a set of black overalls to put on, but nothing small enough for Sam could be found. A young trooper, called Hopkins, only about four years older than ourselves, drove this fifty ton colossus up onto the training area with Meyrick standing in the tank commander's compartment and the two of us with our legs dangling through the radio-operator's hatch adjacent. This young driver then showed off a tour-de-force of skill as he sped neatly through the crash gears across the rough terrain.

Next it was my turn. I got myself into the seat, and listened while the driver explained about double-declutching and flicking steering levers to negotiate the gears. I made a total hash of it, only once getting cleanly from 2nd to 3rd gear, and soon gave way with shame.

By the time I was done, Sam was going apoplectic with frustration. Resignedly, Meyrick got down with him, and settled on the steel slope next to him, while the driver took over the commander's station above. There were lengthy discussions, another cushion was cannibalised from the turret, and so we waited. Hopkins jumped down onto the ground and lit a cigarette. Then the tank suddenly started up again, and he had hastily to throw the butt away, and leap aboard.

The tank crawled away, missed the first gear change, got going again and then progressed smoothly up the box. Coming down, another gear-change was missed, then we got going again. Hopkins smiled next to me, "Staff *must* be having a bad day. Bit out of practice." But things began to improve markedly and soon we were progressing across the flat ground almost without a glitch.

Finally we stopped, and the Staff Sergeant appeared up beside us: "Bloody amazing that boy!"

The driver double-took: "You mean, Staff, that was 'im driving?"

"Yes. A natural, *and* he can hardly reach any of the controls. Shove across, Hopkins!" Meyrick took over the head-set and mic, while the driver transferred to the operator's side next to me: "Driver, advance!"

Sam then took us on a full circuit over some of the roughest parts of the area. As we approached the famous Knife-Edge, where the tank drives up and lurches over a sheer thirty foot high earthwork, Hopkins shouted across to his commander: "You must be joking, Staff!"

The other grinned and shouted back: "Trust me – I'm a doctor!" He halted us thirty yards short of the obstacle, gave some instructions to Sam on the intercom, and then we were off. As we roared upwards, keeled over, then raced down the other side, I just could not believe this was happening.

Then Sam drove us back into the hangar and, under intercom direction, manoeuvred the beast backwards neatly into its bay. After that, something slightly embarrassing and unmilitary occurred: as he climbed out, flushed and covered in dust, Sam was beaming. He threw his arms round the waist of his burly instructor, looked up, tears in his eyes, and said: "Thanks so much, Staff: that was the superest day of my life. Oh my, what a machine!" All the tank crews had gathered round and were smiling and clapping.

Gently the staff sergeant detached Sam: "Well done, lad! Come on, time we made tracks. Captain Lockhart'll be wondering what's kept us."

I took off my overalls; we shook hands with Trooper Hopkins, thanked him and departed.

The *Mercedes* was already parked outside the Museum when we arrived, and the owner was languidly reading a magazine and smoking another cigarillo. I got to the car first and blurted out, "We've had an absolutely brilliant morning: Sam's been driving us round in this tank, and ..."

Staff Meyrick interrupted me, "*Excuse* me, Sir! Little late, Captain Lockhart, Sir. Got a bit keen, we did. Haven't made it even round the Museum yet."

The cavalryman ran his eye over Sam's dusty appearance, "So, how did we do, Staff?"

"Let's just say, Sir, that, if he ever joins *my* regiment, he can drive me into battle *any* hour of the day or night." He saluted, turned on his heel and left us.

We raced back to Studland in the open top. As we stopped outside the house, Lockhart looked across at me, "So, Eros, what did you reckon about it all?"

I ignored his jibe, "I thought all of that, all those people, were wonderful and amazing. Thanks for arranging for us such a really great experience."

"Yes, they *are* great people – and it's a great life. Cheerio! Great seeing you both. Have fun in Jersey!" With which he started up the car again, turned it round and raced away.

As the car disappeared, Helen emerged from the house. She stared at her son: "I gather you both have had quite a morning? Get upstairs and get showered, then I've got a bit of lunch for us, and I'll tell you what the plan is. No rush."

An hour later she was serving us lamb chops, followed by fruit salad. As we tucked in, Sam said, "OK, Mamma, what's the 'griff'?"

She was silent for a while, then said: "I am so glad you have both had a great first day, but I am afraid it was never going to work out for us here in the longer term, after all. I have always liked Gervaise, but he immediately made it rather obvious to me that what he was looking for was the same sort of companionship, shall we say, from which he had recently become separated. I had to tell him that that was not something that I could ever share with him."

"Nor me," interrupted Sam. "Nor my papa."

"So I have done some phoning, and been down to the ferry terminal: we're booked onto tonight's boat to Jersey, and have got rooms in a little hotel up on the north coast. That was the difficult bit: the whole Island's booked solid, I gather. And I had to find a hotel that would take a dog. We must hope and pray that everything works out. But I need to make a clean break from all of this right away. I do hope you both understand."

"Sounds great, Mamma. Sounds like we're eloping."

Helen and I shot a look at Sam.

"No, Sam," she said rather firmly. "We're *not* eloping, as you call it; just making a clean break."

"It's OK, Mamma. *Relax!* I'd better go and look the word up in the dictionary."

CHAPTER 3

Holiday Idyll

After we had repacked the car, we spent a couple of hours wandering about Corfe Castle, then drove the short distance across to Poole. On the way Helen told us what she knew about Jersey. "It's got miles of beaches and rocks. I gather there's a Go-Kart track, Sam. Four cinemas. Shopping's a bit cheaper. A big leisure centre with a pool and roller-skating and things. This hotel we only got into because they had had a last-minute cancellation. All the rooms have got TV with two of the channels in colour. We'll have to ring your parents, Mark, when we get there so that they'll know about our change of plan."

"Sounds good, Mamma!" Then, feeling he had sounded unconvinced, Sam added, "And Flash thinks so too."

But I was delighted: in my selfish way – our elopement as my percipient friend had called it – promised everything I could ever have dreamt of. "I've never been to Jersey," I added, "But I've heard great things about it, and I am really looking forward to everything."

Helen summed it up: "Chance to relax, at least."

We joined the car-queue at the terminal, checked in and then investigated supper at the café. But we all agreed it looked awful, so decided to wait till we were on board. Then there was the excitement of driving onto this new-fangled roll-on/roll-off car ferry. Sam was intrigued. I wriggled excitedly: it all sounded really exciting, better and better.

Soon we were aboard and settling down to an excellent meal. What was less pleasurable was that we were setting off into a continuation of the previous night's storm with high winds and almost tropical rain. Helen, fortunately, had booked us a cabin and we lay in our bunks as the boat pitched and tossed. I felt dreadful and was appallingly sick, but she and Sam seemed unaffected. Helen was a Florence Nightingale, holding a bag and wiping my face. This was not promoting our relationship at all, I thought.

It was still wet and windy, but I caught my breath at the enchanting view as we finally descended to the Chalet Hotel at Bonne Nuit, and I was glad to stagger straight into bed and recover, even though it was still only 8 a.m.

Helen had one room with a big double-bed, and Sam and I had the next door room with another big double-bed. Both rooms had doors out onto the corridor, plus another door into a bathroom between our two rooms. It was muggy, and I collapsed into my bed in my underpants and Sam jumped in beside me wearing that impish look of his that could only mean one thing: I immediately spotted the lump predictably visible in his gold silk Y-fronts. "Now, Sam," I said firmly, "let's get one thing straight, please: you *are* going to behave yourself ...!" He gave me his little-boy-mournful look, but then put his transistor radio against his ear while I settled down to recover my equilibrium. I knew my words had immediately hurt, even maybe disappointed my friend, but he was most definitely *not* on my agenda. I slept.

I woke up at lunchtime feeling ferociously hungry. As soon as we had eaten, as the weather was still bad, we drove into St Helier to watch a film – as Sam was a film buff, he always had a host of films up his sleeve that he was desperate to see. We then had supper in a restaurant in St Aubin's before heading back for an early bed.

Lying there, I could think only of Helen. Trying to sound disinterested, I asked Sam casually, "It's been three years nearly since your dad died like that. Has she really not taken up with anyone else at all?"

"Nope!" he countered briefly. "I'd know at once if ever she did."

"But we all need *someone* to love, surely?" I persisted.

"And be loved by," retorted Sam, slightly pointedly. "She's got me, the business, the dog – and you, of course. Seems plenty to me." He was lolling back against his pillows watching the television, every so often jumping out of bed to switch between the channels or change the volume, while I lay on my back, dreaming of Helen. Casually he started to stroke my chest. "Gosh, you are getting superly hairy, you know. I wonder if I'll ever get like that." As he seemed to need this thing so badly, I let him stroke my bare chest and belly, but when he started to move lower, I had finally to tell him 'No'. I knew that I was a spoil-sport and genuinely wished to show him some gratitude for the kindnesses he and his mother always showered on me, but quite clearly what he most desperately wanted just was not for me. All I could think of was how I could insinuate myself back into Helen's arms: would providence come to my aid a second time?

As I turned these selfish thoughts over in my mind, I became aware that Sam had turned off the TV, but was still sitting there bolt upright in the dark. On an impulse I reached out to touch his hand. It was wet: I reached up in the dark and touched his cheek. He had said not a word, but was just sitting there crying silently.

I have never felt so unutterably wretched. I sat up, stacking the pillows behind my back, then drew his slender frame over to me in the dark, placing my cheek against his. "Come on, Sam: tell your oldest friend what this is really all about! Go on, tell me how you really feel!" Little by little he began to shake, as all the hurt and crying came out.

Hesitantly he began to tell me, "It is just that I *do* love you, Mark. It's that simple. I always have loved you more than anyone and more than ever I can say. It's not so much me wanting to have sex with you – well, OK, maybe I do – one day perhaps I'll show you some wonderful things – but not nasty bummy sex. You are so big, so strong, so – so manly. I don't want anything from you: I just want to feel you really close to me, holding me, loving me, and, well, I sometimes wonder whether you love me even the slightest bit. You just never show it."

I said nothing for a long time, just taking it in, marvelling at his warmth and tenderness, despising my own macho shield. I stroked his smooth chest gently: under the fingers of my right hand I felt his little heart beating. I too loved this lad more than I could say or define; yet I had not the slightest clue how to express these feelings.

After a while, on instinct really, I turned my head and kissed his damp cheek. Slowly, in his turn, he turned his head towards me, and even in the dark I sensed our eyes lock. He found my other hand, slowly drew it towards him, and slipped it into the top of his golden silk underpants until I held his stiffened member. Almost without realising it, I was kissing him full on the lips. As I kissed him, and fondled him, I felt him shudder as the fluid coursed into my palm. "Bless you, Marcus!" he sighed, "For being the most loving friend that any guy could ever want to have around."

After a while he got up and slipped off his underpants; then went to wipe himself off. That done, happy and relaxed, like a little puppy-dog that is full after dinner, he curled up against me and was soon asleep.

A little later I too got up to wash my hands. Suddenly I felt rather great about myself, understanding just a little bit more about the nature of that mysterious love that is possible between men. Just for once my attempts at sleep were not tormented by my longings for Helen.

I woke finally to the sight and sound of a Portuguese waitress bringing two huge English breakfasts to our bedsides. "Where did these come from, Sam?"

"I just rang Room Service and ordered them: big-uns for us two, continental for Mamma," he responded importantly. "I felt you, we deserved them." I looked into his eyes. But he was giving nothing away. As we prepared for the day Helen was not quite as serene, steady and unfussed as the Helen we were so used to. She was suddenly seriously agitated over one matter, "Mark, it is *vital* we call your parents and let them know where we are – in case they try and reach you in

Studland. That's the only number they have." I nodded, attaching no great urgency to what she was saying ... Me? I was *really happy* for once in my life: I had managed to make Helen happy and her son happy. Tonight I was determined to make Helen happy again. Why need I share any of this with my parents? Helen finally got through to Germany, but there was no answer.

That day it grew hotter and hotter. We had decided to make a day of it on St Ouen's Beach. We swam, surfed, cavorted, and snacked while Helen mothered us and tended our every need. And as I lay on my beach towel, I could look at nothing else, think of nothing else but her beautiful body and how I might finally persuade her into my total embrace ... I plotted and plotted and plotted for the night ahead. But it was not to be. Flash had been fidgeting for some time, obviously suffering from the heat. Suddenly it became clear that little Sam, too, had caught too much sun: he started to feel sick and to go hot and cold. We rushed him back to the hotel and Helen put him into her own bed where she tended him all night with gallons of drinking-water, tablets and love. On her reminder I had called home again, but there was still no one there. I gave the number to the hotel manager, who also tried but again without success. "I think they must have gone away," I told her, as we watched over Sam's feverish body.

"Well, we must keep trying to make contact. I have to know that *they* know where we are holidaying."

"I am sure they are not that bothered, so long as they know I am with you."

"Of course they're bothered, Mark!" she snapped. "Any parent would be."

I decided to drop the subject.

By morning the crisis was passed, and Sam was almost back to his former self. "Mamma, go-karting! Can we go go-karting today? Please, Mamma!"

As it was still hot, she was ready to agree. "Do you mind, Mark?" I knew already what we were in for, so off we all went to the go-kart track to the south of the airport.

Completely out of Sam's league, Helen and I were glad to lean against the perimeter fence and watch the master at work. It was not a very taxing course, but Sam was determined, as ever, to test himself on it to the limit. There were quite a few carts on the circuit. Having cast his eye over the fleet, Sam picked the best one he could see when it became free, and launched forth. Then, as another car that he fancied flew into the pit, he would follow it, and switch cars. The manager demurred at first, but very soon he recognised an expert, and between them they ensured that Sam finally was at the helm of his best car. Once he was ensconced, Helen and I had to record his lap-times. He was furious when his machine suddenly stopped out of fuel, running back across the track for a can of petrol from the manager, who was short-staffed and harassed. I got permission to run across to the stranded car. We filled it, I push-started it and then ran back with the empty can. Helen officially recorded the delay as a pit-stop, and then Sam went on tearing round till the car finally ran out of fuel again. Frustrated, he dumped the car and walked back to join us, "Lunch, I think." Helen paid off the manager with a hefty tip, which was gratefully acknowledged.

Then a curious thing happened. Sam was criticising the track to me in, as I felt, a rather boorish and unnecessary way. Having paid, Helen turned and looked directly at us from a distance of at least twenty yards, or rather at Sam. He looked back at her, shuffled and then groaned quietly, "Oh dear. She's right, of course." Then he went over and thanked the harassed manager profusely, shaking his hand and wishing him luck in his most charming, genuine manner. And then we left to find lunch.

As Helen drove, I marvelled at the telepathy that united mother and son. Animals seem to communicate in a similar way; we humans have, apparently, lost the art. There was more communication in Helen's stillness than in her utterances. I simply had to learn how to tune in to this amazing woman.

That evening we went for a quiet swim, and then for a stroll on Fremont above the hotel, and then wandered back for supper. Sam was obviously exhausted and almost fell asleep in the middle of his meal and, soon after, Helen packed him off to bed. The two of us sat watching the television in the lobby quietly respecting each others' company. As we went up to bed I wondered curiously what, if anything, might happen. Other than Helen's motherly kiss, nothing did, and I undressed and curled up next to Sam's soundly sleeping body, profoundly disappointed. Desperately I wondered what on earth I could do to improve my situation – and assuage my aching need. I tossed and turned, but sleep would not come as fantasy relentlessly intervened. Finally I came to a decision: I would go to her and talk my feelings through with her.

Heart pounding, I crept through to her room and knelt by her bed. Then I gently stroked her hair and whispered: "Please can I hold you again, Helen?"

"Oh dear!" she considered for some moments. "All right, Mark, just for a little while, but you must promise *not* to get over-emotional."

I snuggled in beside her. She was wearing a sort of bikini this time. I laid my face against her sweet-smelling breasts. "What am I to do, Helen? I love you so much. And I want you so much, it hurts."

"I know you do. And you're a really nice boy. And I am *very* fond of you. But, you see, you are nowhere near old enough to be getting up to these sort of japes. Apart from anything else, it is actually against the law, anyway till you're sixteen."

I thought about this for a while: "What's the law got to do with anything? You know I am a proper man already. Look, OK, I can't drive till I am seventeen, but my Dad still takes me out in his car on the airfield to teach me to drive." I let this sink in, then: "Why can't you teach me all the grown-up things? So that, when I *am* legally old enough, I shall know how to do things so that I can make girls really happy." Helen was silent. "But, that apart, you see, I do so love you, both of you, Helen. Please let me at least hold you like that night of the storms." By now I was in tears of love, infatuation and frustration.

She was silent for a while holding my head in her hands. Then, after a while, "You may undo my top, Mark. Do not hurry, if you hurry *anything*, I will simply ask you to go back to your own bed. Understand?"

She told me how to unclip the garment from the back and, as it fell away, she turned back towards me, and I kissed her nipples one by one. Then I kissed her on the lips, and she taught me the art of tonguing. Then she kissed my chest. Then she turned again, and I kissed her back and shoulders. Then she led me through an idyllic woodland glade of mutual kissing. Our pulses raced through this eternity of bliss: as I kissed her thighs, I realised, almost casually, that the covering of her secret place was no longer there and so I kissed her most intimate place, snatching at its aroma. Then I pulled down my underpants wriggling them past my ankles. I made myself pause before we began exploring each other again in lip-kissing. Suddenly the moment came when I finally knew that my lover was mine. With a gentle sigh she drew me over her parted legs and guided me into her most secret place. Then, cupping the cheeks of my bottom in her hands, she drew me up deep inside her. Instantly I lost all control and the semen was powering up inside her. "Oh, Helen!" I gasped at the sheer wonder of it.

We lay together for what seemed an age, and I only then realised that Helen was crying. Concerned that I had done something wrong, I stroked her tears gently: "Tell me, why are you crying, Helen!"

She made no reply, but wept and wept. I rolled away to lie beside her and held her close as she wept as if her heart would break. Very slowly, as I held her, her grief subsided. When she was finally still, I spoke again, "Tell me, Helen! Please!"

"I have had no man love me since Peter died – and God knows I have had enough offers. But, as you were loving me then, I felt as if he were in my arms once again, and suddenly

I knew how desperately I missed him." She was reflective for a while. "You were not my Peter; you were Mark. My Mark. But I felt almost as if Peter was there guiding you. Do you mind my saying that? You were so absolutely wonderful, you know: unselfish, thoughtful, responsive and kind." Then: "Is that such an awful thing to say: that you, an entirely different man in every possible way, should have caused me once again to feel love for and weep, finally, for the man I have lost, for the man who was torn from me before I had had more than a quarter of a life with him, the father of my son? Is what we have done so very wrong?"

Responding, as I saw it, to my own selfish needs, what she had said had never even occurred to me. But it was so nice to accept her words as some sort of accolade, "Helen, I think that is the greatest compliment you could ever have paid me. You are a wonderful teacher. A man needs such a teacher."

We lay together for a while longer, sharing the magic. Then: "Now go back to your own bed, old fellow! And, Mark, as soon as you wake up, have a good, hot shower! Don't forget; it's important: Sam has a sharp nose, and will pick up my scent on you at once." As I got out of bed, Flash stepped up to take my place. Then I slipped quietly back to the side of her still sleeping son.

What a truly blessed and wonderful person she was!

The next day this amazing mother organised through the hotel a fishing trip for us out to the Ecrehous Rocks in the boat of a local fisherman who owned a hut on the rocks.

As we walked down the S-bend road to the harbour, Helen stopped to talk to an old lady in a wet bathing suit, who was puffing up the hill. At first I thought her rather old, fat and ugly, but when she spoke she had a clear, cultured voice and a jolly, relaxed manner.

"Who on earth was that?" I asked, once we parted.

"Oh, that is Aunt Maude, Mark. I don't know what her other name is. I gather she has lived in that rattle-trap house of hers next to our hotel all on her own since her doctor husband died before the war. Winter and summer she bathes in the harbour every morning. When the Germans came, and moved everybody out, she refused point blank to go. She *really* sorted them out. They even fired a shell into her house from the gun on the end of the pier. It's still lodged in her skirting: she's shown it to me. In the end they sensibly allowed her to let her stay there. True bulldog spirit: show the Hun who's in charge ..."

Our fisherman was a local from Bonne Nuit, quite young, in his thirties. Flash, who hated water, was quite sure that this particular expedition was *not* for him, but Sam, with his wonderful way with animals, cradled the shaking creature in his arms in the dinghy as Robin sculled us across to the boat. The day was hot once more and the water milky smooth as we chugged out of the harbour. As his fear subsided, Flash put his paws up on the gunwale, and studied the passing sea in some amazement.

First, we went round into the next bay to pick up lobster-pots. Sam nabbed the cork floats with a boat-hook; I hauled up the rounded wicker cages on board and the boatman skil-fully picked out the spider-crabs and dropped them over the side. Very occasionally we found we had hooked a proper crab or lobster of an acceptable size, and he would drop it into a bucket of cool sea-water. Following which he would re-hang some more fish-bait in the pot, and I would lower it carefully over side. Helen held the tiller with the same skill and confi-dence that her son had demonstrated on the go-kart track, and quickly won the owner's approval.

Job done, we motored the five miles or so across to the Ecrehous. As we approached the rocks, Flash jumped up onto the bow decking in high excitement. We anchored, allowing for three hours of tidal drop, and I then rowed us ashore in two round trips in the little dinghy. Sam, cradling Flash once again, commented dryly, "So, all that rowing last term wasn't completely wasted then ..." We were the only people visiting the rocks that day and the peace was total. Our boatman host went off to search for shrimps and limpets. We snorkelled in-shore, lazed on the sand, swam, ate the sandwiches that the hotel had provided, read books, chatted a little, and Flash broke the habit of a lifetime paddling in the sea to keep cool and munching on vraic sticks. All this time I could think only of Helen, her body and her quiet kindness, and how lucky I was to have met up with someone as understanding and generous as her, and a pal as fun to be with as her son.

Late on in the afternoon our boatman decided that his five plastic buckets of shellfish were harvest enough. We carried the dinghy down to meet the rising tide, and then I rowed us back to the fishing-boat. We returned to Bonne Nuit tired and supremely happy.

As we got in, the manager handed me a message to ring my parents urgently. I rang at once, but once again could get no response. I gathered from the manager that it was my father who had rung. I told Helen about this in a fairly throw-away manner, but she seemed un-reassured.

[*I have had lengthy personal heart-searchings about describing in detail this next event, but, after finally tracking Sam down with the motor-racing team he is with out in Italy and speaking to him for over an hour on the phone, he has insisted that what I have written should stand. In his own words "it is relevant and important" to our story.*]

I had paid no visit to Helen that night. Partly my loins were assuaged, but we were all comfortably tired and I had felt that nothing again could compare with that wonderful first Jersey night of our true love. So it was with some astonishment that I woke with the dawn to find and feel Sam snuggling up against me. He was quivering a little, and, as I opened my eyes, I realised he was up on his elbow looking at me with his doe-like eyes. I reached under him, drew him in beside me, and stroked his curly blond hair: "What's up, Sam?"

The words came tumbling out as they always did when he was over-wrought: "You know how much I love you and, well, I just want to show you what it is ... and ... well, my balls are aching again like crazy." Feeling I could cope with things a little better now, I said: "Do you want to kiss again – you know?"

"Oh, more than that, Mark. Much more."

I demurred, fearful what might be coming next.

"Just lie still on your back as you are – close your eyes if you like! – and let me show you!"

"What if your Mamma comes in in the middle? And catches us at it?" I protested rather lamely.

He considered this contingency for a moment. "She'd *never* just burst in on us. And even then I think she would understand ..."

Somehow I doubted it. "OK, but you must *promise* to stop the moment I tell you if I am not hacking it. Promise? And first I must just scoot to the loo."

"Promise!" He fixed me with a look of such infinite love and gratitude. And what he then did, when I returned, I could never have believed.

First, with his delicate flautist fingers he started stroking gently down my chest, over my belly, then over my pants. The contents at once rapidly increased in size, despite myself. Next he made me turn over, and he ran his tongue down my spine to the top of my pants, which he then helped me slide off. Then he rolled me back again, parted my legs, knelt between them, and gazed down admiringly at my parts. "My, oh my, Mark! What a fantastic armoury!" Next he kissed my lips, my nipples, my belly button and then, well, I feared greatly what I felt certain would happen next ...

"Enough, Sam!"

He looked up in some disappointment, "I don't *mind*, you know. But OK ..." He stepped lightly off the bed and slipped off his slinky silk underpants till he was standing there like Cupid, his own wiry little penis erect like a fledgling bird reaching up out of its white nest begging to receive a morsel from its parent. Then he hopped back to kneel between my legs. Slowly he leant forward, looking deep into my eyes. Then he kissed me on the lips, put his cheek against mine and whispered in my ear: "Touch me, Mark! Touch me ever so gently!" He raised himself a little. I reached up under him and gently stroked his tight little scrotum and ran two fingers along the underside of his penis. His eyes, which had been searching so deeply into mine, suddenly glazed over; he gave a little sigh, his back spasmed and immediately I felt his warm semen course up my belly, up my chest and then finally up to my very neck. "Melt-down, Mark!" he gasped, "Bloody melt-down!" He lay there in evident massive relief. "I have waited for this for so *long*."

Much relieved, myself, that this episode had come to a satisfactory conclusion, I felt I had to say something to lighten the moment, face to face as we were, "That was one of your Nuclear Science practicals, I assume, Sam? My, that was an offering and a half for such a little lad!"

Fortunately the little fawn took my gentle jibes in good spirit. "Marcus, you are utterly impossible," he protested. "You did not *have* to say anything, you know. I go through life initiating you into a young man's most gorgeous rituals, and you just go all pompous and belittle my finest hour." He lay back luxuriating in his release. "But, yes, that lot's been nearly three days abuilding, mate – something of a record for me! Enough to father Alexander the Great's entire army, and then some ..." (Sam's A-level subjects elect were to be Ancient History and Mechanical Science with Nuclear) "You don't want me to do the indecent thing, do you?" He gently touched my slackened member. "No, I guessed not."

We lay together a little while longer. Then he kissed me quickly on the lips, got up, sponged himself down in the bathroom. Next, he washed the flannel out with warm water, then returned to wipe down my front. He was pensive, as if he wanted to say something else. But he thought better of it, washed the flannel out again and lay down beside me once more.

There was silence between us. Then, finally, he turned on his elbow again, and looked at me with such infinite love and gratitude: "Thanks, Mark, I've been aching to do that with you for so long – even if you haven't. I promise I'll never push you into doing it again – unless, of course, you want to," he ended impishly. Then, pensive again: "And Mark?"

"Yes?" Suddenly I suspected, and dreaded, what might be coming.

"I know you love my mamma, and I know you have been in cuddling with her, you know." I suddenly felt chilled, and could not prevent a tell-tale blush breaking out. "I have thought about this a lot. And I just want you to know it is absolutely *fine* by me. She needs a man to love her so very, very much; and I cannot think of a finer, nicer, kinder guy for her." I took his hand gratefully. "And do you know what?" Tears began to form in his eyes as they always did when he became even slightly emotional. "I still miss my papa so terribly, and you are the very best dad a guy could ever have. I mean, he *did* say he wanted you to look after us, didn't he?" He kissed me again, snuggled up beside me, just as he had that time years ago in Matron's sickroom, and soon was asleep.

I lay there, my mind in a whirl, only now realising the depth of the waters into which I had ventured. Yet I felt, finally, that I could handle it, and drifted off into sleep, my right arm still cradling my infinitely precious charge.

When I awoke hours later, it was Helen looking down at us with some concern. "You two must have been tired: it's half past nine." I wondered if she had even an inkling of what had passed between us. Maybe she had, for she whispered: "Promise you will look after him for me, Mark, whatever ever befalls?"

I gazed up at her and nodded: "Promise". Something I knew was seriously worrying her, but I could not yet tell what.

"Thank you, Mark. I know you will." She turned away. "I thought we'd have breakfast downstairs for a change. Come down when you're both ready! No rush."

That day had been pre-booked for shopping in St Helier – Helen's day. But on the way she wanted to find Eric Young's Orchid Gardens. Helen had a passion for orchids, she said, and the gardens were famous. After a number of wrong turnings round Victoria Village we finally found the place, and spent a memorable morning wandering around this beautiful place listening to one of the world's greatest living experts. For those who are well-versed in the orchid, its history and its erotic connotations, I need say no more; the Eric Young Foundation still attracts huge numbers of visitors, and, if the reader is not fully aware of these connotations of which I speak, a visit might prove intriguing. Suffice it to say that from my classical education, I had already picked up that 'orchid' was the Greek word for 'testicle'.

Sam noticed nothing, other than commenting favourably upon the scent. But I was immediately smitten and, on an impulse, blew the rest of my holiday money on the orchid of Helen's choice. She chose the very best I could afford, and I solemnly presented it to her.

Next, we did two hours' window-shopping in St Helier buying a few luxuries that were a little cheaper than on the Mainland. Then we took the cable-car up to Fort Regent for a snack lunch. Helen then gave us some money to amuse ourselves while she carried on shopping without the encumbrance of two bored, teenaged boys.

I had this strange, unreal feeling all day as slowly I adjusted to the modified role to which both Nielsens had individually elected me. I do not think that, even one week ago, Helen would have just left the two of us completely on our own in an entirely strange amusement complex. Sam and I felt closer than ever we had been before: he had drawn me totally into their lives to take his father's place, and his mother had made me the happiest and the most fulfilled being that any man could wish for.

After we had swum, roller-skated and spent most of our allowance on side-show amusements, we sat drinking milkshakes and chatting inconsequentially in a corner on our own. Suddenly I heard myself saying: "Sam, how did you know about me and your mother? And when?"

Sam grinned. "My dear old Marcus! My mamma and I have been so close so long that she and I always know everything about each other pretty well straight away, almost without even talking about it. We knew you were not very happy at home, so we just wanted you to be part of us, like my papa said."

I thought about this for a while. "Do you think she knows about you, you know, doing it with me?"

"A bit maybe, not us actually *doing* it together, of course; but I told her some time ago that we had always been more than just casual friends. Why do you think she didn't insist on putting us in single beds? I simply said we would prefer to be together; she would never have questioned something like that." Then he went on: "You aren't the first man I have been with by a long chalk – as I imagine you have already guessed from our last session." He gave me one of his imp-like grins. "Most of the seniors in my house were pretty oafish, and just wanted to rape my bum and clear out – and I was having none of *that*. But there *were* quite a few kind ones who just wanted to share a brief bit of blissikins together. And that was really lovely. And that was why I wanted to share it with you as well. I would have hated to think of you going through life without an inkling of what you had missed out on." He grinned at me again, then turned to gaze nostalgically out over the Bay.

When he looked back at me, I returned his smile: "My dear old Sam! You *were* a randy rascal – I suppose you still are. I don't think I would ever have wanted to hear the details of all your first-year conquests of the house hierarchy." I paused. "But what is it you see in me, for heavens sake? What do you so *want* about me?"

"Everything!" he said simply. "Take your bed-snake for a start: I could throttle that massive boa-constrictor and eat it for breakfast." He pretended to leer.

"Ouch! Steady ..."

"And then it's your face, your juicy lips, your bum, your muscles, all that animal-like hair ... But, all that apart, you're just a *great* bloke, you always have been, and I love you, pure and simple." And then, as an afterthought: "Same things, I imagine, as my mamma goes for."

53

It was totally mind-boggling.

But Sam was still explaining, "You know Grantham in our year? Well, he is my current First Love."

"I don't believe you, Sam," I spluttered. (Grantham was a nice enough fellow, but he was built like an ox and the main support in the second row of our Rugby scrum, and, seemingly, totally unattractive.) "How can you find anything remotely attractive, physically, about Grantham, for pity's sake? How can you even *consider* letting such a rhinoceros anywhere near you, let alone into your bed? Put my mind at rest: tell me it's not true!"

"Oh, Mark, you have so little understanding of these things. OK, Martin Grantham is built like the back end of a bus, but he is a human being and a man assembled like you and me of bones, flesh and blood; and, mark my words, some day he will become ensnared by some incredibly beautiful girl by whom he will have a herd of Olympians. I knew by his manner towards me that he wanted me more than anyone or anything else in the world; yet, knowing his deficiency in the pulchritude department – shall we say – he would not have dreamt of pushing me for anything. When I invited him to come and cuddle me one night, he was overwhelmed with gratitude. He turned out intensely gentle and just enclosed my sylph-like body within his enormous, superbly muscly frame. You would not credit the size of his sex-bits: his foreskin was like a sou-wester, his cock was massive every whichway, his scrot was like a tennis-ball, and when I teased the tip of his strawberry with my tongue, he avalanched like the Matterhorn. And all the time he was weeping with gratitude like a child. And do you know what he said? He said: 'Sam, I shall never wank again. It must always be *with* someone.' I told him never to swear an oath he could not keep. But he's just a lovely, humble guy. And I love him."

I decided it was time to divert the subject.

"Gosh! But tell me," I went on, deeply curious, "Don't you like girls *at all*? I mean with blokes it is a bit unnatural ..."

"Marcus! *Of course I do!*" he retorted, obviously still frustrated at my evident lack of a proper understanding. "I would leap into bed with almost any girl that would have me *right now* – if only to find out what it's like. But what girl would take up with a scrawny, baby-looking, little guy like me? I just would not know where to start to get a girl going – whereas with other chaps, if we fancy each other, it's sort of dead easy. And nice; *God, it can be so nice*. The trouble is: it's these bollocks of mine, you see: somehow I keep needing to do it all the time; and jerking my rocks off night and morning – and after lunch even – gets a tad unfulfilling and would lead anyone to needing *something* a bit extra eventually, I would suggest. And what's unnatural about two chaps liking what they're at? You see two men in a pub drinking together because they like to, don't you? That's not thought unnatural, and, for heaven's sake, that stuff's *poisonous*; yet nobody minds if you're over eighteen or something, unless you go rolling around drunk. Frankly, me, I'd rather be having it off with some other guy than that. I mean: 'A sensation shared is a sensation doubled', or some such thing."

"Ooh, yes! I certainly agree with you there ..." Helen had taught me that.

"One day, in a few years, I expect, I'll start getting bored of other fellows, and girls will edge up to the top of my fantasy list. Or maybe not. But I hope so, because I think I'd like to have a wife and a son of my own one day. A daughter even, I s'pose."

I pondered what he had said, marvelling at his easy, thoughtful approach to such things, so different from my own austere upbringing. But now I wanted to completely change the subject.

"Sam, listen! Enough about you and your rocks! About me, me and your mamma: you're *sure* you don't mind me being with her some nights, and not with you?"

Sam was silent for a while. "A bit envious sometimes perhaps, but I accept that, despite my best efforts, you're not 'funny', like I am. But my mamma, much more important, she's *so* happy now. She has been so *lonely* on her own since Papa got snatched from us like that. It's been agonising – for both of us." He leant towards me. "But Mark, promise me you won't desert us, not ever! Shake on it?"

We shook. And, as if on cue, Helen appeared at our table

to collect us. She had just had her hair done: she was looking radiant, and I longed for her embrace more than ever before. She sat down with us. "Phew! King Street's now *packed*. You could walk on peoples' heads! Tourists, mostly in an unwholesome state of undress, all enjoying themselves ..." She wriggled her nose.

Then casually, and without a moment's hesitation or embarrassment – and as if from half a mile away she had known what we two had been speaking about – she said, and more to me than to him: "You're sure, Sammy, you are quite happy in your own mind about Mark and me?"

Sam got up, and plonked himself down on her lap. "Mamma, of course! I want you to be happy. Mark is utterly gorgeous and makes you happy. And he is my very best friend. And Flashy is happy too." So simple can such things be.

She bent down to kiss the hair on his head. "And you're sure that you understand this thing about Mark's age?"

Again Sam nodded. "Stuff that, is what I say."

Thus it was, with that all cleared up and out in the open, we headed back to the hotel. While Helen was parking the car, I asked at Reception for a little vase, headed up to her room, and placed the orchid on her dressing-table.

As I lay in bed that night thinking about her, I did not feel I could leave Sam's side before he was asleep, and for once he seemed unable to sleep. In the end I found a handkerchief, reached across, found my friend's aching member and did for him what I knew he wanted. He sighed with pleasurable release, turned away from me and manoeuvred his naked little body backwards into my arms. Despite my floppy member being against his bottom, he knew I would never be tempted to try to enter him: I loved him, I loved his dear body, but for me it was always in an entirely non-sexual way. But I could now understand totally those feelings that can develop between men, even if I myself could never give overt manifestation to them. I was just not made that way. Yet I kissed the nape of his neck, and he stirred appreciatively. And so we fell asleep in this embrace.

I awoke as the dawn was breaking over the distant French coast. In a way all at once I felt cheated. Sam had separated away from me and was still sound asleep, and I suddenly realised that I had never *actually* seen my beloved lady unclothed. All our ecstatic togetherness had been conducted in total darkness. I lay there, assembling my fantasy, the longing for her growing by the second. How would my goddess look in all her naked beauty? I tried to picture her ecstatic look as we finally came together? In parallel, I recalled Sam's triumphant ecstasy, his gasping cry of "Meltdown!" at his moment of coming ...

I got up quietly so as not to disturb my friend, sprayed myself discreetly in the bathroom, and then tip-toed in to Helen. She was awake – did she ever sleep? – smiled invitingly, and lifted my side of the sheet. I pulled off my pants, erect and ready. Appropriately, the sun, too, was just rising in a clear sky out of the sea, the orchid by the window in its pot erect next to it. I pulled back her sheet and blanket completely and gazed a while at her totally naked beauty, the smooth, unmarked skin of her face and body, her beautiful breasts with their delicate nipples.

I reached and turned the soles of her feet towards each other, then gently pushed them up towards her, so parting her deliciously inviting thighs. This at last seemed to be the ultimate fulfilment for me of the fantasy lady on the strip of magazine that Sam had given me back at school, and, as I gazed down at her, my member almost erupted. "Oh God, my goddess! Are you really the most beautiful being in the whole world, Helen?"

"Maybe for now, Mark," she breathed, "for beauty is in the eye of the beholder. Passion, you see, is but transient."

"For me it is for ever, Helen."

"Passion is never for ever, oh great one. Only love."

By now I was kneeling in the diamond so formed between her thighs and her legs. Without preliminaries I leant forward and she slowly guided me into her deliciously warm cavern. "Try to hold on just a little bit this time, Mark!" she whispered. "I know how difficult it is, but hold still and see if you can wait. I was afraid you were never coming back, and, oh dear, God forgive me, I needed you so badly, you dear sweet boy. It's seeing your orchid here that will always remind me of you. That was such a very thoughtful, beautiful present …"

Slowly she started to move, breathing, then soon moaning quietly. Together we swam like dolphins in a pool, jiving rhythmically in unison. I thought I had already experienced every possible joy known to man, but what she taught me that morning was on an entirely new plane. Our actual concourse cannot have lasted so many minutes; yet it seemed like an age of bliss and contentment, as we breathed, kissed, tongued, rolled and loved. When finally we separated, I knew that the world was a most wonderful place, and that Helen was the unique author of my happiness.

As we lay there in the afterglow I asked, "What did you mean, Helen: passion is transient, love is for ever? I adore you; I always will."

She said nothing.

"Please explain, Helen! Please!"

"No, Mark, I do not yet feel it would be appropriate."

"But you promised to teach me *everything.*"

She was silent for a while longer, then: "You need to understand, Mark, that passion is but the first stage of what could – in our case only theoretically, of course – become a lifetime's union. True love is what emerges from the rubble of spent passion. Many never attain it. Peter and I did. Many believe they have attained it, and then, twenty years later sometimes, the devil creeps up on them unawares turning love to hate, and their tried and tested union breaks up in flames. I am immensely happy that you should adore me, Mark. But you must never say that you love me; even if you *think* you do. For *they* will not let us."

"They?"

"'They' is the law; 'they' is society. Our wonderful time together can have only one outcome. I dread it for both of us. I just want us to be all happy together while we can – before they come down on us like wolves in the night. When they do, you will be made to discover, in fire, the true difference between passion, love and loyalty."

When I awoke, still in Helen's bed, I found myself staring up at the startled face of our Portuguese chambermaid. Almost as if out of routine, she had slipped in unannounced, so as not to disturb Helen, to place the continental breakfast on her bedside-table. As the girl retreated, I dashed through the bathroom into my own bed, so that, when, a few minutes later, she came in with our two huge English breakfasts, all she saw, as usual, were the recumbent heads of Sam and me, still asleep.

As both Sam and Helen had been asleep, and so had not noticed what had happened, I decided not to say anything about the incident, and it drifted from my memory. But I subsequently discovered that the maid had not been deceived, and had taken it upon herself to go and report Helen and me to the Hotel Manager. He, on the other hand, had reprimanded her for her lack of discretion, stressing to her in Portuguese that, how paying guests conducted themselves behind the closed doors of his hotel, was of no concern to either staff or management. As it turned out, incensed at the rebuke, she refused to let the matter go – and ultimately lost her job as a direct consequence.

But I was aware of none of this at the time; and our days proceeded in happiness and contentment.

CHAPTER 4

Arrest

An idyll can be transformed into a nightmare on an instant. The blow when it came was monstrous and cruel. It came like an evil dragon in the night searing, thrashing and wounding every creature in its path. Helen has found herself able to forgive; but it was years before I finally managed to forgive those who set events in motion, those who rode that beast and those who ultimately so crushed the very breath, almost, from our lives.

Each morning I would creep into Helen's room about an hour before dawn, and together we would watch the sun rise over the French coast and she would teach me new and wonderful ways to perfect our love-making. Then, well before breakfast arrived, I would slip back to Sam's side. Usually he was still asleep, but if he was already awake with the TV on, he would always give me a little knowing smile, and sometimes snuggle up to me in shared companionship. But he was too mature ever to comment.

Thus it was at about 7 a.m. on the ninth day of our Jersey holiday, that I was lying in bed beside Helen, enjoying the afterglow of our quiet contentment. As we lay there sharing the final moments before I left her side, out of the blue things suddenly began to happen at a sledge-hammer pace.

We heard a mild commotion in Sam's room adjacent. Voices: a man's, then a woman's, a sleepy Sam, querulous, protesting. Helen went rigid beside me; I felt I had been punched in the solar plexus. The dividing door burst open. The woman came in first and walked round to Helen's side of the bed, and the man followed to mine. Flash barked at the intruders twice, then dived under the bed in terror.

The man spoke first: "I am Detective Sergeant Philip Lucas and this is Detective Constable Jeanette Gallichan. We have instructions to follow up on information that a crime may have been committed." He pulled out a note-book, "Are you Master Mark Edward Hallam?"

Before I could respond, there was a high-pitched screech from our intervening door. Sam was standing there in his silken briefs: "Don't you say one damned word to these bloody people, either of you! Mamma, Mark, send them away! They have absolutely no business in here at this hour ..." His voice faded as a rather large lady, who had hurriedly appeared behind him, put a burly arm round his chest and swept him back. "You'll kindly take your hands off me, Madam ..."

I have to hand it to Sam. His fuse is short and his reactions immediate: always the racing-driver, he had sized up the situation in an instant and was coping on instinct. My fuse, on the other hand, is long and slow-burning. I anger slowly, but when I get angry, I get very angry indeed.

I had some inkling what was happening by the very fact that Helen beside was clearly numb with terror. But I had some vague idea of my legal rights, and was determined to counter-attack with calm and aggression. In retrospect I like to think that I fielded the situation as I would catch and dispose of a rugby ball in the face of the menacing horde bearing down on me.

Naked in bed next to Helen, I made the two police officers a short speech: "I do not know what you two mean by invading our privacy in this manner. Nor, frankly, do I care. If you seriously wish to pursue any matter, I suggest you both go down stairs and ask the management to get you cups of coffee. We will join you in the dining-room when we are dressed – and not before." This seemed to work: they left.

I lay back in bed, quaking.

Helen finally uttered: "Oh my God!" Then lapsed into silence.

I got up and went back to Sam's and my room, and started showering. While I showered, my mind was working fast, trying to work out precisely what 'crime had been committed.' How could anyone have discovered, or even guessed, that a) I was only fourteen and b) I had been sleeping with Helen? I decided that nobody could have known. I went back into Helen who was still lying there pole-axed: "Love, come on, we have to get up and face these blighters."

She was distraught, "Oh, Mark, I am so sorry. You are going to be in quite a bit of trouble and I, well, I shall probably finish up in prison. And I will not see you or Sam for years."

I replied with more conviction than I felt: "Not a chance! They can't know about us. And, if some blessed law has been broken in our case, the law is an ass, anyway. Come on, you get up and put on your best, and let us see these plods on their way!"

While I was talking, Sam reappeared, looking triumphant: "You should have seen me! – it was lucky it was only 7 a.m. – there I was standing in the main Dining Room almost starko being embraced by this social worker woman ..."

Helen interrupted: "Social worker, Sam?"

"Yes, can you believe it, she said she had come to see that I got properly looked after? I thanked her politely for her interest, told her that her help was not required. Then the other two came down again and told her to let me go."

"Oh my God!" said Helen for a second time.

"Mamma, don't worry! Mark and I will see these troublesome busy-bodies off the premises, won't we, Mark?"

I was immediately reminded of our pact, "Of course we will."

Buoyed up by our naive 'Boys Own' enthusiasm, Helen finally pulled herself together, and dressed herself up as only Helen can. Then, as a united team set for battle, we entered the dining room chatting noisily about out plans for the day, as Flash settled himself in his accustomed place just outside the dining-room entrance. The room was still deserted except for the officials, who were sitting huddled round a table on the other side of the room in total silence. They looked across as we came in. Helen sat down while Sam and I moved to an adjacent table. We then invited the three others over to join us.

They were clearly on the defensive and keen to get this tricky situation cleared up as soon as possible. But Sam and I, having regained the initiative, were having none of it. I picked up the menu, "The full works, Sam, as usual?" – a full fry-up was the very last thing I felt like at that instant – "Me too. Coffee and croissants, Helen? Sam, perhaps you can get ordering? Oh, and order another round of coffee and some croissants for these good people too, will you?" Sam headed for the kitchens. "And Sam, let's have that coffee-jug in here right away, eh?"

I turned to the intruders. "We've all had a bit of a hectic start to our day, haven't we?" I smiled benevolently, determined to maintain our strategic advantage. "It's OK, we quite understand: you've got a job to do; not a problem. But a bit intrusive and heavy-handed, don't you think? Not quite what one wants when one is having a really great Jersey holiday?"

The police sergeant finally spoke up, half apologetically, "Routine procedures, I am afraid ..."

"I don't envy you your job, if that is how you have to 'proceed'. Mrs Nielsen was really quite upset, you know," I replied, genuine anger just beginning to re-emerge.

Sam appeared with the coffee, topped up cups and then sat himself between me and his mother.

"So!" I said, finally broaching the matter: "I don't know if or how we can help you, but we will if we can, obviously."

The police officer pulled out his note-book again. "As I said earlier, I am DS Lucas, this is DC Gallichan and this is Mrs Claire Amy from the Care Centre. We have been asked by the Mainland Police to locate and identify Mrs Helen Nielsen and Masters Samuel Nielsen and Mark Hallam."

Sam went wide-eyed: "Well, here we are, at your service! But *why*, for heaven's sake?"

Sergeant Lucas was obviously uncomfortable: "Complaint about a suspected abduction, apparently ..."

Sam's eyes grew even wider, "*Abduction?* Of whom? *By*

whom?" Sam was doing so well, I thought I would let him get on with it.

The sergeant paused for a moment, braced himself, then said quietly: "Mrs Nielsen has been accused of abducting Master Mark Hallam."

I exploded, "*Are you serious*?" This was so absurd and unexpected, I felt almost relieved, and, as I looked across at Helen, she clearly felt a measure of her burden had been lifted too.

"Quite serious! It would appear that a Wing Commander Hallam of RAF Bruggen in Germany contacted the Mainland police in an effort to locate his son."

It was now my turn to be pole-axed. So, it was my own idiot father who had so utterly thoughtlessly brought ruination upon our idyllic holiday.

Helen jumped in at this point: "Obviously, Sergeant, there has been some serious misunderstanding. Yes, I am Mrs Helen Nielsen and this is my son. And this is his school-friend, Mark Hallam. We changed our holiday plans and we tried, by numerous phone-calls, to let the Hallams know in Germany. Obviously without much success. But that is all there is to it. Mark, have I abducted you?"

I shook my head, still knocked sideways by this turn of events: how could my own parents have done this to me? How could they have been so unbelievably *stupid*?

Sam stood up, anxious to conclude a very nasty situation as quickly as possible: "Well, that's all right then, everybody, isn't it?"

There was an uncertain silence. Finally the sergeant spoke up again, "Certainly, on the face of it, there does appear to have been some misunderstanding. I shall need to go back into Town and consult with the Mainland police by phone. When do you plan to leave the Island?"

"The day after tomorrow, probably." Helen replied. "The boys are due back at school then."

"That's all right then. We will leave you to enjoy the rest of your holiday. And if anything else crops up, we will know where we can get in touch with you. I would like to apologise again for what must certainly have appeared to be our rather heavy-handed manner this morning."

"Heavy-handed?" Sam exploded "Dawn-raid more like!"

Sam never knows when to shut up ...

The three officials trooped out just as our fry-ups arrived. Sam and I shook hands with a triumphant "Yes!" and then set to with a will.

While we ate, Helen remained withdrawn and uneasy. After some minutes Sam said: "What's up, Mamma?"

She forced a bright response: "Oh nothing, Sam! I've just had a bad shock, that's all; and I thought you both handled things brilliantly, needless to say. But I think I would really rather get on back home. Would you two mind if we took the ferry back tonight?"

Sam looked at me, and I nodded. "Sure, Mamma, to hell with them all, let's pack up and wagons roll! But can we have one more quick burst on the Go-Karts?"

We packed our cases, Helen rang the ferry company to change our tickets and we were fortunate in finding that they still had space for us on the night boat. Then we thanked the hotel owner for all his hospitality and help, checked out (apologising for our precipitate departure) and drove up to the Quennevais Kart Club. While Helen, Flash and I watched Sam racing round with crazy determination, I held her round her waist.

She voiced her fears: "They are not stupid, you know, Mark. They saw the two of us naked in bed together. Why that poor Sergeant did not arrest me there and then I shall never know. But they are going to be back. You can be sure of it."

"We have done nothing that either of us need ever be ashamed of," I replied. "We have done nothing wrong. I simply love you."

"I know you do, you dear, wonderful person. But the law will say that I *have*. And the world is chock full of pernicious people whose one purpose in life is to enforce the law, right or wrong. No, that's a wrong thing to say. Of course the law of the land has to be enforced; it exists to protect society. But I suspect that this could become the sort of 'juicy' case, where lots of busy people will relish getting up on their high horses, identifying evil where none exists, and, of course, turning a tidy penny in the process. Our relationship is an utterly beautiful thing; yet 'they' will seek to besmirch it."

"Helen, I – Sam and I – will never let them lock you up, Helen. That is a promise." I kissed her openly. "Oh, my dearest love, I am so very sorry: I could absolutely kill my father. What an *idiot*!"

After the Go-Karting, we had one last swim at St Ouen's, followed by lunch. Then, to kill time before the evening ferry, we toured the German Underground Hospital. As we walked round the subterranean works and marvelled at the highly organised slave labour that had gone into their construction, together with all the pictures associated with Hitler and his dire mob, Helen remarked wryly: "There you see, boys, what can be achieved by people set (in genuine innocence in most cases) on a totally misguided path. They killed millions of mad, handicapped and physically disabled people; they killed the Gypsies and they murdered the Jews, six million of them. And why? Because a gang of thugs, under the pretext of some crazy ideology, convinced them it was the right thing to do, and then backed that up with laws and guns ... Any country could have got enmeshed in all of that. As it happened, it was the Germans, and, unfortunately for the rest of us in this case, the Germans have always proved themselves highly organised and efficient." And suddenly she was crying again.

Next we took Flash on a final tear-around up at Grosnez on the North-West point.

Then Sam insisted we take a final supper at Helen's favourite restaurant in St Helier to cheer her up. But even "Moules Meunieres" in Bath Street failed to raise her spirits, and we boarded the ferry a silent trio.

This state of affairs annoyed Sam greatly: as far as he was concerned, the crisis had been brief and unpleasant, but was now over, following our famous victory. He just could not understand why Helen and I were taking so long to recover ourselves. But Helen knew, and I suspected, that there could be yet much worse to come.

Although I have since spoken with Detective Sergeant Lucas, I can only record in vague outline what had happened down at the Jersey Police HQ at Rouge Bouillon. The previous afternoon the Jersey Police had received a request from the Mainland Police to locate a woman and her son who, it was claimed, had abducted another boy from a Dorset house and fled to Jersey. DS Lucas had been given the job of locating and apprehending them, possibly the most exciting mission in his entire career in the Jersey force. It had not taken him long on the phone to track us down, and he had then decided that the only way of being sure of not losing us was to catch us in our hotel before we could leave for the day. When the group arrived at 6.30 a.m., the only person around was a somnolent hall porter who, without further thought, had given Lucas our room numbers. In total disregard of proper procedure, he had decided to barge straight in.

Little was said as the car, carrying the dispirited trio, accelerated up the hill out of the Bay. Mrs Amy was the first to speak up, "I am not a bit happy about any of this. I was called out at some unearthly hour to 'help deal with a most urgent matter', you said. And it looks as if I, the Care Service and the Police have been made complete fools of by a couple of toffee-nosed public schoolies. Yes, I shall certainly be making a report."

"It is not quite over yet, I don't think," Lucas said. "Wing Commander Hallam is still pacing about on the Mainland, as I understand it, and ..."

Constable Gallichan interrupted: "And what I want to know is what was the Hallam boy doing in her bed? I don't think he had anything on, and nor, I'd bet, did she. There must have been quite an age difference."

"Quite!" replied the sergeant. "I was about to make that very point myself. And it is not just age difference: Hallam, according to this, and if my sums are right, is under age. I think we just may be able to turn this whole thing round. If we handle it right, Inspector Riddle in Bournemouth may yet end up owing us one for ensuring that he comes up smelling of roses instead of the manure hitting the fan. I frankly don't believe those two cocky lads were really quite so sure of themselves as they tried to make out. Particularly Hallam. Do you know how old the telex description said he was?"

"No! Do tell!" his companions chorused.

"Fourteen!" In the silence that ensued he let the implication of this bombshell sink in.

"I don't believe you," said Mrs Amy finally. "OK, the blond cherub's fourteen all right, but not Hallam. I would put him down nearer seventeen or eighteen."

"At least," agreed Constable Gallichan. "My, oh my! But I don't see how we can prove anything. We can only report what we saw."

"Quite!" replied the sergeant again. "Case dead – unless the cocky bastard admits it. And I for one would not put it past him. He's fourteen all right; they are boarding schoolmates. And from what I know of those institutions they will be of a very similar age."

On returning to his desk Lucas was on the phone to Bournemouth for over an hour. He then rang the hotel to arrange an interview room to be made available for that evening. The receptionist promised to ring him back.

This time, Lucas vowed to himself, we have got some solid information and instructions, and we are going to get this damned thing done right! Two hours later the hotel proprietor rang back: "I am not very happy with all this police activity up around my peaceful little hotel. Sure you can have a room, if you insist, but it had better be handled with a sight more discretion than this morning's episode."

"When do you expect them back?"

"Who? You mean the Nielsens?"

"Yes, of course." The sergeant was rapidly losing patience.

"I don't. They checked out this morning. Thanks to you lot, probably: three nights' business gone down."

The sergeant was beside himself, "They did *what*? Why in hell did you not let me know at the time? No, don't answer that; you are the typical, discreet Jersey hotelier; don't even remind me! Do you by the slightest chance have the UK registration number of their car?" There was a silence. "Well?"

"I'll have to ring you back on that."

"Look, you have that number on your register, I need it; it's vital."

"I'll ring you back."

Two hours later, having heard nothing, he rang the hotel again. An efficient-sounding receptionist answered, checked the register and came straight back with the precise information he needed.

He then phoned the ferry company and cross-checked the Nielsens' updated booking.

Next he got a trace through the DVLC in Swansea.

Finally he called Inspector Riddle in Bournemouth. The latter was out on a case, and was not responding on his car radio.

In the end it was after 6 p.m. before Lucas's phone rang. "The Nielsens are doing a runner with the other boy," he reported to the inspector, "They will be boarding the ferry in three hours. I can have them stopped, but I need to know now. Otherwise they're your baby."

"Shit! I'll call you right back."

Lucas waited an hour, and was just beginning to think that he was well shot of the whole unpleasant business, and donning his coat to close out on a particularly bad day, when his phone finally rang again.

"It's been decided that we'll field them and handle it this end," Riddle told him, "I reckon it's thank you for all your help, and sorry you've been troubled."

"You appreciate, I am sure, that the only offence, if it was an offence, was probably committed at this end. We do also have a claimed witness for you, a Mrs Maria de Jesus, housemaid working at the hotel," the sergeant told him, almost casually.

"Ah, that might prove handy, you never know. But I reckon it will all rest finally on the boy's evidence, and they are wheeling out the big guns this end to handle it. No disrespect to your boys, of course."

The sergeant stood down the patrol car he had alerted, and left the office. God, what a day! He wondered, as he stepped into his own car, what would now become of the case. He asked himself if the Mainland police fully appreciated quite what was about to hit them. He smiled: from the side-lines he could acknowledge a sneaking admiration for these two 'public-schoolies'. And Mrs Nielsen *was* a very attractive woman ...

Unlike the outward trip our journey home was across a mill-pond. But there were no cabins left, so we two boys had to lie on the floor while Helen dozed upright all night. She has described that night as one of the worst of her life.

We decided to miss out breakfast on board. Having descended, bleary-eyed, to the car-deck, we drove off, never dreaming that the sword of Damocles was about to fall with such uncompromising swiftness. Helen drove up the ramp and into the Customs shed. Then, after a brief exchange at the check-point, continued slowly on with the line of cars. Suddenly a man in a grey raincoat motioned us to stop, and Helen wound down her window. He glanced round at the three of us: "Mrs Nielsen? Detective Inspector Riddle." He discreetly displayed his warrant card. "I wonder if you would mind stepping out of the car for a moment and coming across to the office?" He smiled disarmingly at Sam and me. "You two can wait here. Shouldn't take long."

As Helen slowly picked up her handbag and got out of the car, I looked round at Sam, "Cue to move?"

He nodded, reached forward and took the key out of the ignition: "Lock your door and stick tight with Helen! I'll follow up in a tick!"

As I got out, Sam was out of the back-seat into the driver's side and poking around in the foot-well. Just as Helen and I, side-by-side, were following the policeman across to the open door, a photographer appeared from nowhere and flashed a picture of us. He was immediately pushed aside by another plain-clothes man guarding the door.

Inside was a small room with a table and a couple of chairs. In the corner stood another, older man drinking from a plastic cup and smoking a cigarette. It was only as the inspector closed the door behind us that he realised that I had accompanied Helen. "I thought I told you to wait in the car?"

I flushed, anger beginning to rise, "Yes, officer, I believe you did. I would not, however, dream of leaving this lady on her own. Perhaps we could rustle up another chair? Even two more maybe?" I drew the chair back for Helen.

The inspector looked at me surprised. To compound this, there was a sudden explosion of high-pitched noise outside the door: "I *am* going in ... If you don't get your hands off me, you oaf, I shall start screaming 'child-molester', and this pressman here can take another picture ..." The door burst open and Sam appeared in full volume. "Sorry about that, Mamma: just securing the car." Ostentatiously he flicked the keys in the air, then put them in his pocket, and sat down on the end of the table.

The inspector looked questioningly at the man in the corner, who carefully laid down his cup on the window-sill, and disappeared into the adjacent room. After a moment he appeared with more chairs.

I thanked him, took two from him, brought them both round to our side of the table and offered one to the inspector, who reluctantly subsided into it next to Helen. I then gave the other chair to Sam who, still sitting on the table, put his feet up onto it. Next I collected another chair which I sat astride with Sam behind me. Happy that we now had wrested back some control over the situation, I looked expectantly at the official. As he failed to respond immediately, I decided to open the proceedings, "Any chance of some cups of something, Inspector? I imagine you may have had yours, but we were on our way to get some breakfast."

Again he looked across towards his senior, who spoke to someone in the adjacent room.

There was a further silence broken by a knock on the door. Our guard put his head round, "Customs want their car moved, Sir; it's blocking one of their exits; holding up the flow."

Sam spoke up, "Tell them: sorry, no! It leaves when we leave. And kindly be careful not to get the dog all stressed: he is easily upset." (As Sam was speaking, I urged Helen quietly not to say one word.)

The man looked questioningly first at the inspector and then at his senior, but, gaining no encouragement, closed the door behind him.

Inspector Riddle suddenly exploded, "This is outrageous!"

I raised a hand, "Quite, Inspector! It is utterly outrageous. I would put it even stronger: I would say it is more like 'harassment'." I stood up. "Frankly, we are beginning to find these early morning 'dawn raid' routines just a shade tiresome. Now, perhaps you could tell us what it is that you want, so that we can all get on with our lives."

"It is a little awkward," Inspector Riddle began, a shade defensively now. "The investigation we are dealing with concerns Mrs Nielsen alone …"

"Somehow I doubt it, Inspector," I said. "Come on, what are the charges?"

"Oh, at this stage there are no charges. We are simply following up on information that a crime, or crimes, may have been committed, following a complaint made by a member of the public. We believe Mrs Nielsen may be able to help us with these enquiries."

"There are no charges," I echoed, "I remember Sir Thomas Moore said that to Sir Thomas Cromwell shortly before Henry VIII ordered his head to be chopped off. But good! Even so, obviously Mrs Nielsen will be answering no questions without her solicitor being present. In the meantime, however, it might be helpful if we were made aware of the nature of the complaint." The inspector took a deep breath, not at all happy with the current turn of events.

"In the circumstances, I think it would be better if the written complaint were presented to the lady concerned." He made as if to hand a piece of paper to Helen, but I snatched it from him, and, before he could stop me, I had read it. I cannot remember the exact wording but something to the effect that 'It has been alleged that Mrs Helen Ann Nielsen abducted Master Edward Mark Hallam. Further, that she had sexual intercourse with him unlawfully, him being a minor, on or about the 20th August 1977 and on sundry other occasions ...'"

"And the complainant," I asked. "Who is the complainant?"

"A Wing Commander Hallam." Cups of tepid dispenser tea now arrived.

"I thought we had put that canard to rest with Sgt Lucas in Jersey, Inspector? If we could have got hold of my father, I could have reassured him myself, and we could put a stop to this particular nonsense here and now."

Inspector Riddle smiled for the first time, and I felt a cold chill: "Your father is waiting outside now to take you home."

This I had not bargained for; but it was something I should have thought of: "Oh really! Good! Well, he had better come in then, hadn't he?" I was not looking forward to facing my father.

"No, I don't think that would be appropriate. But the Chief Inspector here will take you through now."

"Later maybe." I was not rising to any bait to break up our trio. "You said 'crime or crimes'? Rest assured no one has abducted me. What else?"

"Could you confirm your age, please, Master Hallam?"

"My age is whatever age my father told you it was, Inspector."

The inspector reddened, but said nothing. Then he turned to Helen, "Mrs Nielsen, are you prepared to be questioned informally, in private – without a solicitor? It might expedite matters."

"No, she's not!" Sam and I chorused, and Helen shook her head.

"Do you have a solicitor you can contact?"

"No, she hasn't." Again we chorused, and again Helen shook her head. There was a silence.

It is terrifying how, in human affairs, a situation which one believes one has fairly well under control can suddenly up and run away! In moments we were in mayhem, and everyone was shouting at everyone else.

First I asked, "So what happens now?"

"What happens now," declared the inspector, "is that you are returned to your father." He turned to Helen: "And I must ask you, Mrs Nielsen, to accompany me down to the police station where we will arrange a solicitor to be present during your further questioning."

"No way!" burst in Sam, "And what happens to me anyway while all this is happening?"

"You need have no worries on that score, young man," replied the inspector reassuringly, "We will see that you are properly taken care of."

"Taken into care!" Sam was screeching. "Where my mother goes, I go! Only at the point of a gun are you taking me into any squalid care-centre!" (Sam watched a deal too much television, in my view.)

"And wherever they go, I go," I chimed in, "Until this preposterous business is sorted out."

"Neither of you boys have any choice in the matter under the law. You *have* to do what we say and go where we say ..." the inspector was shouting now as well.

Sam jumped down from his perch, snarling: "You can go and stuff your beastly law. Just you *try* us, Officer, Inspector!" He sped across to the main door, wrenched it open, and shouted, "Mr Pressman, get yourself in here, fast!" The rather scruffy cameraman pushed straight in past the security man, off-guarded for a second time that morning, and stood there looking a little bewildered.

Sam grouped the three of us, glaring at the police inspector, "Now, separate me from my mother and take me into care, would you? Just you try!" The photographer snapped his flash-bulb and fled.

Helen started crying openly now, and I bent down to try and comfort her.

At this moment a familiar figure suddenly appeared in the doorway of the adjacent room: it was my father. He beckoned to the chief inspector who followed him back into the other room.

There was silence, broken by the main door opening yet again and a frustrated Customs official putting his head round: "Inspector, OK you have a job to do, but so have I, this car out here has *got to be moved!*"

"You've got a key-set you can try, haven't you?" snapped back the frantic police officer.

"Tried that, no good. It won't start and the transmission's locked up solid. Can't make it out."

"God, man!" said the despairing inspector "Just wait a few more minutes, will you, and we'll try and sort this thing out finally ..." The Customs man turned on his heel, shaking his head, cursing, and left.

My father now re-appeared with the chief inspector: together they took control of our battlefield. The latter spoke first: "Wing Commander Hallam has suggested we quieten this thing down with some proper breakfast for the three of you. Our Mrs Freeman here will go round to the restaurant at the front with you in your car. In the meantime he will try and make some arrangements on the phone."

I looked at my father: I knew him well enough to know that he would play fair. Moreover, he knew that he had been mostly responsible for getting us into this sorry mess, and that it was therefore up to him to try and straighten things out. I looked at Sam who by then had taken over the comforting of his mother. And then nodded to the chief inspector and to my father.

A motherly-looking Mrs Freeman now appeared from the back room. Then we all trouped back to our car. Sam withdrew a bolt from somewhere behind the clutch; then joined Mrs Freeman in the back. Driving very slowly, in a total daze, Helen followed the care-lady's rather uncertain instructions past containers round to the front of the building. We found the restaurant, and, almost sick with hunger born of stress, Sam and I ordered massive meals. Helen was eventually persuaded to have a coffee and what passed for a croissant in this dire establishment.

"I've already had my breakfast," intoned the care-lady, "You can call me Dotty, if you like; most people do. What a noisy business! I could hardly believe my ears: you were really giving the inspector a time, the two of you ...!" She stopped to pull some knitting out of her bag.

"So, tell us about this institution they want to bang me up in, Dotty!" Sam gave her one of his impish looks – he clearly had taken an instant liking to this woman.

"Oh, I doubt if it'll ever come to that, love."

"No, go on, do tell! Of what does the clientele usually comprise?" mouthed Sam pompously through puffed wheat.

She parried the question skilfully: "I doubt if they would even let you in. Bad influence, you know. You, I mean!"

"You needn't worry, Dotty," he said soothingly. "Mark and I are off back to our own current institution in a couple of days, anyway."

"Yes, I know all about that one. Makes my point exactly." She giggled quietly.

It was over an hour later that my father finally reappeared with the chief inspector. He drew up a chair with the policeman standing behind him: "Right, listen out, chaps! I have had a long talk with the Chief and spent a fortune on the phone. This is what we have decided is best for all concerned. We will all go up in convoy to the school where I have arranged for you two to clock in a couple of days early. Sam and his mother with Mrs Freeman will lead. Mark and I will follow. And the inspector will follow us in his car. I have arranged for Sir Piers Lampson, a solicitor I know quite well, to meet us up there. Any interviewing can then be undertaken up there as well. There! Any questions?"

My mind was racing. I trusted my father. He was a superbly efficient organiser, and I myself felt fairly comfortable with his arrangements. He would have remembered that Uncle Piers was a solicitor whom I knew and respected.

Sam was less convinced, "OK, Sir, but I *must* be with Mamma at the interviewing, and so must Mark. She is not being left to that terrible inspector on her own."

"Well, we'll have to see about that," said my father. "Mark, tell Sam and his mother about your Uncle Piers!"

"He's not a proper uncle," I told them, "But he is a thoroughly down-to-earth sort of fellow: I would trust him with my life." I knew that neither of us were going to be allowed into that interview-room, and so, I suspected, did Helen and Sam. I decided to risk my father's wrath. "Thank you, Dad," I said with care. I glanced at Helen and Sam, "I think we *will* agree, but on one condition."

He stared across at me, clearly startled by such unaccustomed impertinence, "Go on!"

"Helen is not be questioned by anybody till the three of us have spoken fully *and in private* with Uncle Piers."

My father was shocked and silent for an instant, clearly upset at the lack of trust which my words so publicly implied. Obviously he had no alternative but to agree. But at least Helen and Sam seemed reassured. He threw a glance at the chief inspector.

"I have no quarrel with that."

"Right!" said my father with forced military joviality, "Let's all mount up, then, and get this show on the road!"

I am not sure, in retrospect, that Helen was in any fit state to drive that day. The 100-mile journey up to the school seemed interminably slow. Following along behind her, for a long while my father and I exchanged not a word. Finally he could contain himself no longer, and broached the subject that was uppermost in his mind. "I have to ask you, Mark, did you at any stage share a bed with that woman?"

I suddenly felt as if my father inhabited a different planet: his attitude, his words, his standpoint had no relation to my own reality.

"Father, 'that woman' is Helen Nielsen; and the three of us have just had a wonderful holiday. I am sorry: so far as I can see, I have done nothing wrong. However, as what we did on our holiday appears to be in legal question, you will forgive me if I wait to discuss it with Uncle Piers, and with no one else. You will not persuade me. Do you mind if I turn on the radio?"

He stiffened and I thought for a moment he was going to pull in to the side of the road, get out and thrash me. But, with the car in front and behind, he finally simmered down and just stared at the road ahead, deep in his own thoughts. Some minutes later he turned down the radio and made the following speech in icy tones. "You are my fourteen year old son. For another three years plus you are my *total* responsibility. If you commit a public wrong-doing, it can affect all our futures, your mother's, your sister's, not to mention my military career. Don't you see that?"

"I see that all too well, father – not least ALL our future careers," I replied immediately. "So I just cannot understand why we all find ourselves in this situation at all. So far as I am aware, none of us three have offended anybody: we were simply enjoying a fantastic holiday. Suddenly, out of the blue, all hell breaks loose, the police are snapping at our heels and the press are not far behind. You and Mother had been happy for me to go out with the Nielsens for years. I cannot understand why you have made all this heroush suddenly happen . . ."

We exchanged never another word the whole of the rest of the way back to the school.

We arrived at lunch-time and parked up. As an Old Boy, my father knew his way round the huge school. We followed him in procession through the cloisters to the Headmaster's lodgings where we were met by a group that included him and his wife, my own Master-in-College, Sam's Housemaster, . . . but no Uncle Piers – he had rung to say that he was delayed but was on his way. Facilities were made available, and the Headmaster's wife took Helen under her wing. Sherry, lemonade and sandwiches were laid out and hearty conversation ensued, pointedly unrelated to the matter of the meeting.

To everybody's obvious relief, Uncle Piers finally arrived, bustling and friendly, and lightened the underlying depressed atmosphere with his mild banter.

The Headmaster and my father disappeared with him into another room. About a quarter of an hour later he reappeared with my father, and then took Helen, Sam and me through. It was obviously his main study – I had never been in there before – with comfortable arm-chairs and a view overlooking his glorious garden. It was also furnished with ornate chairs round a circular table on which pen and paper had been laid out. Finally he turned to us: "Mark, Sam, after you two are completely finished here, you are to go back to your houses with your respective house-masters immediately. You are in no circumstances to speak to anyone at any time about any of this – I should warn you that we anticipate a problem with the press – any such contact will be treated as the ultimate disciplinary offence. Do you both absolutely understand me?"

"Yes, Sir!" we chorused.

"Right, I will plonk your inspector down in front of my television until you are all good and ready for him, Mrs Nielsen. No rush! Good luck!" He departed, closing the old oak door behind him.

Uncle Piers sat the three of us down and, with his inimitable chuckle, spoke first: "I have only a vague inkling, Mark, what sort of pickle you have got yourself into. But, the rumour, shall we say, is that you and Mrs Nielsen were caught, as they say, 'in flagrante delicto' ... I am not here to make any moral judgements; I am here to advise you in matters of law in as friendly and helpful a way as I can. If we are not very careful, this could turn into something of a cause célèbre. If I am to act effectively, I need to know absolutely everything that happened down to the minutest detail, however personal and embarrassing this may be. Mrs Nielsen, I understand why your son remains by your side, but are you sure that he wants to be in on all of this?"

Helen pondered this for barely a moment: "There have never been any secrets at all between Sam and me. Sam, you must say that you are content to stay."

Sam stretched out his arms round both our shoulders: "You know how much I love you both. You bet I'm staying, if only to be sure that Mark's Uncle Piers *is* told absolutely everything, and he understands that we are as one over all of this."

"So be it!"

The story of our idyllic Jersey holiday took the three of us nearly two hours to tell: the change of plan, the abortive phone-calls to Germany, the night of the thunder-storm, Helen and my growing love for each other, Helen's need for support and affection, Sam's desperate need for a father-figure, our pact, the dawn-raid by the Jersey police and our precipitate decision to return home – everything we told him, everything except those two most private of moments when Sam and I had kissed each other and later made love. That we spared him.

Yet Uncle Piers was so astute, such a good listener, that I know, from a subsequent conversation, he had already guessed that some very intimate things must have occurred between us two boys. He had taken copious notes, and listened so totally that when we had finally finished, he asked very few questions: "First, can you assure me that you both never made love anywhere other than in Helen's bed? Helen never came through to *yours*?"

"Definitely she did not!" Sam and I chorused.

"Second, Mark, how and when did you become aware that under-age sex was illegal in this country?"

"Helen told me very specifically that first time," I assured him.

"Third, when those Jersey police burst into Helen's hotel room, were you two doing anything, if you get my meaning?"

"No!" I said, "We were just lying there half asleep." Helen nodded.

"This is a very difficult question to ask both of you at once." He paused. "Given the chance, would you see this relationship continuing, or is it an affair that you expect to, has, or will soon pass? Mark, first."

"I have pledged never to desert Sam. I see myself as being a husband to Helen and stepfather to Sam," I said immediately.

"When the law allows, you mean?" continued Uncle Piers. I nodded.

"What are *your* intentions, Helen?"

"Yes. Mark is no longer a boy; he is a man. I love him from the depths of my heart, and I wish him to be a stepfather to Sam."

Sam stretched his arms round both of us again. "And it's what I want too, more than anything."

"Right! Good!" concluded Uncle Piers. "Before we face Mr Law-Enforcement, I need to clear up with your father, Mark, about these abortive phone-calls you and Helen made to Germany: it could become important." We waited for him to go on. "I am sure you boys understand that there is no question of either of you sitting in on this interview? It will be just Helen, me and the inspector. If, and only if, the inspector wanted to speak to either of you boys – and you are not obliged to speak to him – would you be willing?"

"Of course I would, Uncle Piers!" I said immediately, "Anything, absolutely anything, to help Helen!"

"Sam?"

"Sure. Of course. Let's get on with it! But I'd much rather be in there with my mamma."

Uncle Piers smiled. "Sam, he may not be the world's most sensitive of men, but he does have his job to do. You must all understand that we have to start cooperating fully with the law, if your mother is to get through this disaster in one piece. Let's face it: so far, from what I gather, there has been precious little cooperation from either of you two boys. You have to recognise that the game is now up. Oh, and Mark: I need hardly say this to you, but you must admit nothing."

I was beginning to feel increasingly depressed: I knew that Uncle Piers was right, and that we could not be in better hands. Yet I recognised, too, that Sam and I had relinquished all control of our situation and were back to doing what we were told. I felt my new-found manhood ebbing away, and my anger with it.

"So, Helen, you stay here with me! You two report straight to your house-masters, and be on call in your rooms! I will be calling you both back anyway this evening once Helen and I have finished with the police."

I hardly glanced at my father as Sam and I passed through the other room. We then went our separate ways. I said a couple of words to my Master-in-College on my way to my room, and then started to unpack the bag that my father had brought over from Germany and had already left there for me. I had never felt so despondent in all my life.

Yet worse, much worse, was to come.

Soon after 5 p.m. the Matriarch-in-College looked round my door to tell me that I was needed back in the Headmaster's rooms. As I started to leave, she grasped my shoulders in a show of some kindness: "Brace yourself, lad! Things, I gather, *could* be better!" ['Matriarch': school title for 'house-mother']

I ran through the ancient pathways and corridors up to the room where we had all come together at lunch-time. The same assembly was still gathered there talking sombrely as if awaiting the start of a funeral service. The Headmaster greeted me quietly and showed me back into the room where we had laid bare our hearts earlier in the day. It smelt uncharacteristically of vile, stale cigarette smoke. Uncle Piers was standing against the high marble mantelpiece. Sam was kneeling beside Helen, and he was sobbing his little heart out.

"Over here, Mark!" Uncle Piers pointed me into a chair at the circular table and we sat down facing each other, out of earshot of the others. "Now listen! News not good, I am afraid, old chap. The police can get very rough once roused; and they have been mightily roused in this case. As things stand, they propose to throw the book at Helen. OK, I am not here to blame anyone; I am here to point out the facts and the consequent state of play, and to do what I can to ameliorate the situation. So far, I am bound to admit, I am not doing too well. If it is any consolation at all, I estimate things could not be worse, so possibly they can only get better." He paused. I waited. Sam was a little quieter now. Helen was looking like death. "This is what is happening," he went on. "It has been agreed that I shall look after Helen till tomorrow morning, so at least she will not have to spend the night in a police cell. I shall then take her down to Dorchester in my car for arraignment before the magistrate. At which I am fairly confident I shall be able to obtain bail till the CPS decide whether to put her on trial ..."

"Trial?" I hissed dumbstruck. "So they *are* going to charge her? What with, exactly?"

"I hoped you would not ask that: you don't want to know," Uncle Piers replied. He looked across at Sam, then scribbled some sentences on a note-pad, which he passed to me.

They read:

"In the worst case, choice from some/all of:

ABDUCTING A MINOR
LEWD/INDECENT CONDUCT WITH A MINOR
EVADING ARREST

"Do not even utter, Mark! Sam does *not* know yet ..."

The world swam before my eyes and I thought I was going to faint. What sort of appalling trouble had I got this most wonderful and gentle of all mothers into? I realised Uncle Piers was speaking again: "The first and last charges I am confident we can deal with. Talking to your father, the first should be accepted as a simple mix-up, and any human jury would grant that none of you had any incentive to continue your holiday after what Sam has so rightly termed that 'dawn-raid'. But the second charge could be made to stick unless it is very astutely handled. All right it is an unspeakable degradation of what you both feel for each other, but English law, rightly or wrongly, takes a pretty dim view of it."

"But what did Helen say to the inspector?" I asked.

"She behaved with a marvellous dignity and control, and said exactly what I had told her to say. She explained the first and last charge; she denied the second. But I have little doubt that they will still bring all the charges; that is how the thing works."

"But surely any jury will believe me," I said, "If I am the so-called 'victim'?"

"You are missing something, don't you see – or rather three things, actually: *if* they prosecute Helen, you will be the prime prosecution witness. Yet you can't be made to give evidence; and if you do, you are not old enough to give it under oath." Uncle Piers paused again. "From a legal purist's standpoint it promises to make quite an interesting case, but we are going to need a pretty nimble barrister if Helen is to get away without a severe sentence. I have two possibles in mind, but whether we can get them is another matter."

"Jail?" I interrupted his flow.

"Even jail. That, or suspended. We have to face the possibility. Now, I want you to say goodbye to Helen, and then take Sam off. Helen, indeed all of us, are relying on you to help see him through the next few days and weeks – maybe even months. You will have to be very strong, strong *and* silent."

"When will this trial be?" I asked.

"Don't know. There may not be a trial. But, if so, as early as possible, if I have anything to do with it. Hopefully even this term. Now off you go, and let me get on with briefing the staff outside: our biggest problem may be tomorrow's press with that wretched cameraman skulking down at Poole ferry terminal this morning. They get just everywhere."

I walked across and picked up the dejected Sam. Together, both now in tears, we embraced our beloved Helen.

"Thanks, Uncle Piers, we know you are doing your best for us." We shook his hand with genuine warmth.

"Try not to worry too much, the two of you! Things never turn out quite as black as they may first appear. I'll let you know what happens tomorrow."

To take our minds off things, my father had offered to pick Sam and me up next day and take the two of us to the nearby Waterpark for a day on the flumes.

My immediate instinct was to refuse anything that my

father was offering, but Sam said: "Oh, yes, please; do let's, can't we, Mark?" So I was not about to refuse. I knew that, second to sports cars, Sam just loved the adrenalin rush of these tortuous, high-speed water-slides: given the chance, he would go roaming the country to sample them.

In fact, it turned out a really good day, and a welcome relief from our ongoing trauma. I became aware, too, what a thorough insight it was giving my father into the close bond that had been wrought between Sam and me. He had already noted how close Sam was to his mother. Taken together, he must now have gained some inkling of the magnitude and the unfairness of this process he had so carelessly set in motion.

When he dropped us back at the school, the news was that Uncle Piers had persuaded the magistrate to grant Helen bail on the one condition that she made no attempt whatsoever to make any physical contact with me, the 'victim'. The relief for the two of us was palpable. Yet I knew not how I would survive without her closeness and embrace.

The school had also got off lightly, at that stage anyway, with the press. On the morning following that terrible day, only one tabloid newspaper had picked up the story from the local paper, with the headline:

MUM IN LOVE-NEST WITH
PUBLIC SCHOOL BOY (14)

Next to this they published the Poole photograph of Helen, Sam and me, failing to indicate, incidentally, which of us was her lover – although it must have been obvious, I suppose.

The accompanying scoop was almost non-existent. And the school, fortunately, was not due to open till the following evening. There was suggestive gossip amongst the boys, of course, on the day following their return, but few linked the story either with Sam or with me. It then died for 'lack of oxygen'.

CHAPTER 5

The Trial

The rest of that term was for me an agonising mental torture, as I am sure it was for Helen and for Sam. What I was enduring in every waking moment was as physical as El Cid going into battle against the Moorish hordes with the arrow shaft impaled in his back, as portrayed in that new epic film with Charlton Heston. In my sleep my yearning for Helen was drowned in her sorrowing tears.

Without specifically raising the point the three of us took this ban on physical contact between Helen and me as not precluding letters and phone-calls; only these occasional communications maintained our respective sanities.

Helen came to take out Sam for lunch every alternate Sunday as before, but I could never join them. As a mark of public unity and defiance, Sam invited me to join his year group for Boys Lunch on the first intervening Sunday. As we entered the Dining Hall side by side, all the boys applauded us – nor did his house-master discourage this: rumours had surged round the school, exaggerated, of course, but mostly positive and supportive. After lunch Sam and I went up to his room. I sat at his desk while Sam threw himself down on his bed, telling me how his mother was coping. "She's so damned tough and dignified," explained Sam, "but obviously, inside, she's worried sick."

"You must tell her not to feel guilty. That is vital," I replied. "I keep telling her that in our phone-calls."

"She knows that, and it's easy to say. You know and I know that she has nothing to feel guilty about. But trying to persuade her of that ..."

We met together like this on many subsequent occasions

that term. Sam's earlier boyish sexuality towards me was already giving way to a less demonstrative mutual love and respect: he seemed to have grown up in a hurry and was bearing our secrets with quiet fortitude. Once, as he lay there, while we listened to flute music on Radio 3, he commented, "It's a funny old law this, you know ..."

"By that you mean what, Sam?"

"I mean, just *look* at it! Here we are, three perfectly straightforward and normal people – responsible citizens, I hope – going about our daily lives, neither offending nor harming a soul: and suddenly a whole load of these pompous busy-bodies decide to crucify you, me, and my mother, all in the name of some fatuous law they've thought up. It's mean, and it's bloody crazy. It's worse than the Middle Ages. In the Middle Ages, for heaven's sake, girls were married and having babies at twelve, with boys of thirteen making it all happen ..." He was silent for a while. "All this trouble of ours is because of some faffing law designed to deter dirty old men in beige-coloured rain-coats with a predilection for fondling little boys' cocks!" He burst into tears, something he did less often these days. I got up, sat down on the edge of his bed and held him close once again, content in the knowledge that I could make some small recompense, at least, by affording him this outlet to his grief.

Half-term was a further torture for me, being spent mostly working in my room in Germany in a self-imposed exile from my family; the possibility of a trial was stacked as a barrier between me and my parents now, and discussion of that I had already specifically ruled out.

I devoted my life with single-minded fanaticism to Sam, to study and to rugby. I was barely sociable, and I scarcely cared. I made it my aim to raise my academic level from 5th out of the 250 intake in my year-group to 1st – anything to block out the grating hurt.

My house-master and I had always held each other in the highest mutual esteem. In total confidence I shared with him all my doings, miseries and fears. He had warned me that a trial was now almost inevitable. Eventually, he called me in to tell me officially that there *was* to be a trial – Helen had already told me in a brief phone-call the previous evening – and the trial date had been set for mid-November. Then it was postponed to early December, because Uncle Piers could not get the services of the barrister he wanted until then. I ground my teeth – slap in the middle of end-of-term exams! Then it was postponed yet again till the first week in January; I prayed it would not change again.

I achieved my first place, not by a few marks, but by a mile. Only my house-master knew the basis for my phenomenal result, although my other tutors probably guessed. In the process I did, in fact, hugely increase my mental store of English Literature, and researched into the way the language was spoken in Chaucer's day.

At the end of term Uncle Piers dropped by unexpectedly. We sat in my room: "I am sorry I can't take you out to lunch, old boy! Nobody knows I am even here – except your man Teddy. [Master-in-College] I am not here. I never was here. OK? I cannot be seen with you, as I have heard on the grapevine that the Prosecution may be going to ask you to testify in court. I shan't coach you, obviously, but *they* probably will. If so, my advice is to be compliant, demure, and youthful during rehearsal, so that they feel confident of putting you on the stand – it is vital they *do* put you on the stand, of course, so that you can wreck their case. Then, once on the stand, be as grown up and mature as you possibly can. You have got to sell your case, Helen's case, to the jury. Without putting too high a price on it, you are probably the only one who can save her. I am sorry to load so much onto you."

I nodded wearily.

"You need to give it a fair bit of thought beforehand, Mark, as I am sure you have already realised. To that end I have brought you a couple of basic law books which you might consider skimming through during the Christmas holidays. It's a vast subject, of course, but, like anything else, it helps to get tuned into the law-man's way of thinking. I've flagged up a series of pages you might read. As important as convincing the jury, don't forget, you have to convince the *judge*.

Pity there's no such thing in England as a woman judge – that's a laugh. I have no idea who our man will be; all of them are first class brains, but a few of them have bees in their bonnets about some things. And under-age sex is a promising candidate for just such bee-keepers ..."

I did as he said; apart from anything else, it gave me an excuse to keep out of the way of my family over Christmas. The more I read the more interested, even intrigued, I became. Overnight, I began to fancy myself as a lawyer and to wonder if this might even be the direction that my future career might take.

On our return to school, I went straight across to Sam's room. I found him in a sombre mood. It had been difficult from back home in Germany for me to communicate in any meaningful way with Helen, and I gathered from him that she was depressed and resigned to her fate. I tried to pass onto him some of the legal ammunition I had picked up, but he was impatient with my new-found enthusiasm. Suddenly he burst out, "Whose side are you on anyway, Mark? Suddenly it's all a great game to you! It is our lives these blighters are playing with, you know."

"Of course I realise that, Sam," I snapped back, disappointed by his attitude, "More, I hope, even than you, but I am rapidly learning in this life that the best chance you have of beating people is by joining them."

"Yes, OK, sorry! It's just that I *hate* this whole thing *and* these bloody people and all their dreary works ... It is all such an unnecessary interference: all I want is for it to go away and be all over and done with, and we three to be together to get on with our lives." He threw his arms round me in despair for his first good cry that term, and I held him for dear life.

After a while he cheered up: "Sorry, mate! I really must brace up. This whole thing has been making me, and Mamma, feel so alone. Where do we go from here then?"

"I gather the Defence may want to get you to say something useful in mitigation, if you are so willing."

"Of course. You wait: I'll tell 'em."

"If you do, Sam, you will blow your mother clean out of

the water. I gather you must answer only Yes or No to each question, with a minimum of embellishment – no loose cannon stuff," I urged him. "Are you quite clear about this?"

"If you say so. OK, I'll try."

"I most certainly do say so. You *must*, and absolutely no messing about and going off on your own tack!"

Two days later I was informed by my master-in-college that I had to go up to Lincoln's Inn in London for my Prosecution interview. I could have made my way up to the Prosecutor's office quite happily on my own, of course, but, for the sake of appearances, I asked if my matriarch could escort me. Initially he was a bit startled by this request, but trusting my judgement, he agreed. She was more than happy to.

Thus it was that the first impression that the Crown prosecutor, Mrs Annie Coleman, had of me was of an older-looking, but fairly insecure, school-boy. I was not entirely surprised that a woman had been picked to prosecute; I already knew that Uncle Piers had obtained the services of a lady defence lawyer for Helen. (And a lady she was, Lady Jemima Fanshaw – "Don't underestimate that name, Mark!" he had said on the phone.)

Mrs Coleman obviously had a number of other priorities that day and kept us waiting for nearly an hour, but in the end she touched down beside us, bright and cheerful. "Sorry to keep you both hanging about; let's go out for some lunch. I know just the place." The three of us piled into a taxi, and in a short while she was paying it off outside an all-day fast-food outlet. I looked at my matriarch, and it was as much as we could do not to burst out laughing; the least I had expected was one of the smarter city restaurants.

Even though I suspect we were none of us much enamoured with the place, I took a childish pleasure in promoting an inappropriate range of items of varying ghastliness for each one of us. The place was busy, so it was a full ten minutes before the three of us were crushed in round a corner table biting into buns, nibbling on chips and sucking at straws.

Mrs Coleman seemed sane and homely enough. She told us about her own Jersey holiday some years before with her own ten year old son and told us a little about what to expect in the courtroom. Then she came to the main point of our meeting. Despite the noise in the place she lowered her voice confidentially: "I know this whole wretched business must have been most unsettling for you, Mark, and all you must want to do is to forget all about it, forget that it ever happened. Our problem is that when a woman, a mother particularly, does something really naughty, she has to be found out, stopped and prevented from ever doing such a thing again. We can only do that if we are able to prove what she did in a court of law. The easiest way of proving it is for the person she did it to to be really, really brave and describe exactly what happened under my questioning in that court. And I am afraid by 'exactly', it means talking about all the rude bits. Like breasts and thingies and all of that ... Do you see? I promise you that no one is going to blame you in any way for what happened."

I nodded gravely.

"Tell me, have you seen any of these courtroom dramas on television?"

I nodded again, quoting some current examples.

"Good! Well, you and I together have also to convince both judge and jury that you are a truthful person. The reason I have asked you to come up today is to meet you and talk to you. I have to make sure that I believe you *are* a truthful person, find out what really happened, and then see if I think I can guide you in such a way that you will convince the court of the truth of what you have to say. (We have to work as a team, you see.) And also, unlike grown-ups, I cannot ask you to swear on the Holy Bible, and, again, unlike grown-ups, you do not *have* to be questioned in open court."

I nodded for a third time. "I quite understand."

"The big problem is: do you think you are big enough and brave enough to go into a witness-box and answer out loud – so that everyone can hear – questions from me about what this woman did to you in Jersey, questions you may find very rude and embarrassing? And without completely breaking down on me half way through?"

"I think so ..." I replied uncertainly.

"Good!" She took another reluctant bite from her bun, paused, then: "So she *did* do some things to you, didn't she?" I suddenly realised that our Prosecutor had most skilfully led me into a simple trap, and that I was about to fall headlong into it. I had to think fast.

After a moment she said: "Look, I promise: I am a mum like I said. Of course this can't be very nice for you. But I really need to know: did she do anything to you that made you feel sort of guilty or uncomfortable or anything? ..." Her voice trailed away.

The true answer to this critical question was, of course, No! At no stage had I felt either guilt or discomfort. But she knew I had been caught naked in bed with a much older naked woman: what on earth could I say? I was so non-plussed that, for the first time in my life, I was caught tongue-tied and I openly and ashamedly blushed.

Mrs Coleman touched my arm, "It's all right, don't worry, you don't need to say any more, Mark. And I don't think we really need to ask you difficult questions in court either. What I *shall* want to do, however, is to get a signed statement from you that I can make reference to during the case; I imagine you would not have any objection to this? You will not be named, of course."

I nodded dumbly.

"Good, wonderful! I am sorry about this, but I shall need you to come up again for this in about four days time, shall we say Friday? I will call the school."

I was in a daze on our journey back. My stupidity might have already sunk Helen, nor was I getting to say anything in court to save her. This disaster was not something I could share either with my matriarch or with my master-in-College, so that evening I put a call through to Uncle Piers at his home. I was almost in tears, as I related to him the events of the day, but he steadied me. "It's OK, Mark, you needn't be too upset. It could even work our way, actually. I have already heard from Mrs Coleman that she won't be calling you; better still I think I have convinced her she does not need a statement. So, if you are agreeable, we, the Defence, shall put you up! But before I can do that, they have the right to question you privately."

"Oh God, Uncle Piers! What do I say?"

"Well, as it happens, we have been having a slightly different problem with Helen. Look, I am going to have to pay you another visit. Your room 8 p.m. tomorrow night. All right? I'll square it with your man."

I was in a quandary all next day. We were getting so near to the trial, and suddenly all the threads appeared to be unravelling.

Uncle Piers was as laid back and jovial as ever when he slipped into my room that evening, but, as soon as he spoke, I knew things were serious. "Let's talk about Helen first – your situation is minor by comparison. Quite straight-forwardly, the problem is this," he began. "You remember how I managed to control Helen at that interview with Inspector Riddle at the start of term? In essence she denied everything. I did not tell you, but after that she was pretty upset. Since then, her resolve has grown that she wants to admit to what happened, in the firm conviction that you and she did nothing wrong. She's mad, of course; she's asking for a jail sentence, but she won't be moved. She has asked that she should plead guilty to the second charge: that's the 'Lewd & Indecency' one. I have dissuaded her from that because what you both did was neither of these. Nevertheless she wants it all to come out to show that, under age or not, in this particular case, your love for each other was 'hallowed and good' (her words) ..."

I thought about this for a while. In a way I felt almost relieved: it seemed, on consideration, the only right and proper way for us to proceed. "I think I would support her in all of that." I thought for a moment, then added: "She is a saint, you know. And, after all, this is all about truth and justice, isn't it, Uncle Piers?"

Uncle Piers sighed, "I wish I could hold up my hand to you

here and now and say that, in my experience, the two always coincide. Were I not in the law business myself, I would be inclined to agree with you both 100%, but my nose tells me that Helen is setting herself up for crucifixion. Even if a jury were inclined to wear it, no judge sitting today would allow them to." He paused to let this sink in. "Nevertheless she is set on this course, and I cannot move her. And it now seems, from what you have just said, that you are not inclined to dissuade her either. Think seriously before you commit yourself!"

I thought for a while. "It does seem pretty straightforward to me, Uncle Piers," I said finally. "The law is trying to show that, because I was under sixteen, that the beautiful and loving relationship, that developed between Helen and me, was 'lewd and indecent conduct'. I certainly do not buy that. And Helen merely wishes to show, with utter firmness, that what we did was loving, beautiful and normal and in no way perverted. Am I right?"

"Yes, you have got it in one."

"Then I most definitely want to support her position," I asserted.

"Even if her and your principles finish up by putting her in clink?" asked Uncle Piers.

"Yes, I suppose, even if it comes to that; and if that is what she truly wants. Something about 'The law is an ass', I heard once?"

"So be it! I admire, even if I do not envy, what you will both have to face. We have a very narrow line to tread, and I must advise you now what you will have to do. Ideally, you should be coached by Jemima, but she is very hectic at present. We have known one another for many years and she has asked me to coach you up."

It was another couple of hours before Uncle Piers finally left my room.

Helen's trial, which was listed in the Dorchester Crown Court, commenced exactly ten days later. It was held there on the allegation that the first offence had taken place at Studland in Dorset. Sam and I were accompanied by our matriarchs. It had been suggested that we need not attend the early proceedings, but we were having none of it: we were going to be backing Helen from first to last. I was to be the surprise Defence Witness. The trial promised to be exciting – and terrifying.

Uncle Piers was his normal laid-back, jovial self, and came to talk to us before we took our places in the courtroom. "Well done, you chaps! I think we have got matters fairly well in hand with both a sane and sensible prosecutor and defence. The only slight fly-in-the-ointment, so to speak, is the judge who is a) male, b) just a shade past it, and c) I suspect 'keeps bees'. Anyway, we'll just have to see. Try not to worry! And, Mark, I am relying on you to keep Sam in order. None of that Poole hero stuff!"

My father had not shown up, but he had already written to me to say that he had 'pressing, military commitments'; he wished me luck. I was a little surprised by his absence as I had imagined that he would have been required to testify on the abduction charge.

Helen took her place as the Accused. She looked sensibly dressed, not over-dressed, and wonderfully dignified, saintly almost – to me anyway.

The jurors were agreed and sworn in without dispute: they were constituted almost exactly 50 : 50 male : female, and two obviously hailed from foreign parts – I found this oddly comforting.

There then followed some rather lengthy legal discussion which meant little to Sam or to me until the lunch-break when Uncle Piers came over with the pronouncement: "Well, that's the first and last two charges out of the way at least: the prosecution has agreed that no 'abduction' had been pre-meditated, nor any conscious attempt made to 'evade arrest'. So now we can get straight down to the meat of the case."

After lunch Mrs Coleman opened against Helen. In essence, she told the court that she was out to prove that Mrs Nielsen, a mother with one son, and widow of some three years, had failed in her duties as guardian and mother by forming an unnatural attachment towards her son's school-friend. That the friend, in ignorance of the law and in response to immature instincts, had allowed himself to be seduced into a series of unnatural acts, which he had been persuaded by the accused (who must have been fully aware of the law) were 'perfectly normal'. As prosecutor she would endeavour to show that, in law, whatever the defence might claim to the contrary, Mrs Nielsen was a degenerate mother and a paedophile.

I watched Helen down there in the dock close her eyes, as the lady in the wig concluded. I could feel Sam shaking. I took him firmly by the arm, drew him towards me and looked at him: "Hold on, old boy, this is just the start! The three of us have just got to ride this out together."

He nodded, but already I could feel he was beginning to weaken.

Next it was Lady Jemima Fanshaw's turn. Sam and I quickly realised what a good choice she was to defend Helen. She was a cheerful, no-nonsense mother herself; also, I gathered subsequently, widowed in early married life. I will try to report her opening speech as accurately as I can. First, she walked over to the jury panel and began thus: "Ladies and Gentlemen of the Jury! I fully appreciate that you have all been pressed some willingly, some less willingly, into the jury service of this case. But you have, in fact, a historically important duty to discharge today. As well as trying a case, we are trying a principle: what you decide in this matter may have implications far beyond these walls." She returned to her place. "The prosecution has just described the accused as 'a degenerate mother and a paedophile' My purpose will be to show that, far from being either of these, she has throughout her life shown herself to be the very best of mothers. Anyone who finds her guilty of paedophilia makes a total mockery of the spirit of that law, which was rightly created to protect the innocent. The defence will show that the so-called 'victim' in this case, was in no sense of the word an 'innocent', except in the sense that he committed no sexual offence, certainly not in his own mind. That he knew exactly the nature of his feelings for the accused, and that, while the accused did not ruthlessly resist his advances, she did nothing, certainly initially, to instigate them. In conclusion, while the prosecution may, misguidedly in observance of the law, describe their relationship as 'wicked and unnatural', we, on the contrary, will show that it was 'natural, loving and wholly good'.

I only just caught Sam's hands in time before he started clapping. We all felt better. What was to be next?

To our surprise the judge adjourned proceedings till the following morning. It was still only the middle of the afternoon. Uncle Piers caught up with us as we were leaving the building with Sam's matriarch. He seemed pleased. "Not so bad so far, eh, chaps?"

"Yes, I suppose so. Great! Thanks, Uncle Piers! But why did the judge pack up so early?"

"Quite normal with the old school, I am afraid; they get to a convenient juncture and think they have done a full day's work. No wonder there's such a back-log of cases! Me, I would go on all night, and get the whole thing over and finished with. The trouble is that the jury get either bored, or mentally overloaded; it is a fine line that the judge has to draw. Don't worry: I expect things really to get moving tomorrow."

My matriarch took us to a wonderful Bed & Breakfast she had arranged just outside Dorchester, where we spent that night.

First to be called to the stand next day, was Captain the Honourable Gervaise Lockhart. He looked rather less overwhelming out of uniform, but dapper enough still in a very expensive suit. Suddenly I was fearful of what he might say. There was no doubt that he had resented me at the time, and this was his perfect opportunity to get back at me – and Helen. Presumably the Prosecution knew this.

Yet, I had to hand it to him. He treated the court with polite but lofty disdain. Had he seen me in Helen's bedroom? No, he had not; he had seen me come *out* of her room, once the storm had subsided. Did my appearance, on coming out of her bedroom, indicate that I had been 'up to something'? Up to what? How on earth was he expected to tell, he queried? Why, in a court of law, was he being asked such an opinion, he wanted to know? The judge nodded at this. And, having effectively diminished the stature of the proceedings in a few short sentences, he was dismissed. I never saw him again. I heard he died some years later on active service. I shall be eternally grateful to him: he could have behaved like a 'shit', and had Helen devoured at the outset. But he did not, and his evidence did nothing to effect the outcome of the trial.

The judge now called for a break, and, in the interval, I asked Uncle Piers why he had even been called.

His eyes widened. "He was called, old boy, because you know, and I know – indeed half the world knows, unofficially – that it was in his spare bedroom that Helen's primary 'offence' first took place. Otherwise we would now be all sitting around, not here, but in the Royal Court of Jersey." He was silent for a moment. "I have to say that I am beginning to fear that that just might have been the preferred venue from the Defence's point-of-view. I have only been over to that little island a couple of times, but, tiddly though it may be, in matters of law it is a shade less hide-bound, and seems to practise a greater measure of common sense – and flexibility."

Next up were Detective Sergeant Lucas and Constable Gallichan over from Jersey. In answer to prosecution questions, Sgt Lucas described how, in response to a call from the Bournemouth police, he and Constable Gallichan had called in at the Chalet Hotel on the north coast that evening posing as dinner guests to pre-identify the Accused, her son and his friend.

"Why did you feel it necessary to burst into their bedroom at six o'clock that following morning, Sgt Lucas?" Mrs Coleman asked.

"Nose, instinct, Ma'am!" answered the detective sergeant with professional pride. "On the way back to the station after supper the evening previous, I had discussed what we had seen with Constable Gallichan and she agreed with me that there was something, shall we say 'odd' in the interaction between the three. The older boy seemed to be behaving more as a father than as a friend of the blonde boy."

Mrs Coleman hurried him on, "Yes, but what *else* did you think might have been going on?"

"We simply guessed that, if he was acting out the father-figure by day, he just *might* be behaving similarly by night. It was difficult to believe that the older boy was only fourteen and a half, actually."

"Please confine your answers precisely to the question, Sergeant Lucas!" the Prosecutor broke in, before the Defence could intervene. "Opinionated asides may not necessarily be helpful. So, what did you decide to do?"

The sergeant fidgeted his feet. "We felt the only way we could confirm our suspicions, as we thought, was by stretching the law a bit and so 'catch them at it'. If we had been proved wrong, we would have looked very stupid, of course."

"And did you 'catch them at it' – as you describe it, Sergeant?"

"Yes, I think we did."

"Without playing to the gallery, Sgt Lucas, can you tell us what exactly you found when you and your colleague burst into their room?"

"They were, er, lying naked in bed together."

"And ...?"

The sergeant shuffled his feet again. "Well, they were sort of just lying there."

"Anything more specific?" asked Mrs Coleman.

"Well, er, that's how they were. But they were definitely naked,"he added hurriedly.

"And how sure were you that they were *both* naked, Sergeant?"

"As sure as one could be without actually ..."

"That'll do, thank you, Sergeant Lucas. No more questions."

Lady Fanshaw rose to cross-examine. "Sergeant Lucas! I am sure everyone appreciates your foresight, persistence and the risk you took with your reputation by the action that you took. Some might have espied even some excess of zeal, but we will not pursue that. Tell us, you mentioned earlier that you 'had difficulty believing that the boy was only fourteen and a half'. Why was that?"

The Prosecution rose: "Objection, my lord: the Defence is asking for an opinion of the witness."

"As it came up earlier in your questioning, I must allow it. You may go on, Lady Fanshaw. But please avoid leading the witness! Re-phrase your question, please!"

"How old did you *think* he looked, Sgt Lucas?"

The man was obviously uncomfortable, aware that he had dug his own grave on this one. There was a pause. "Answer, please!"

"Sixteen, seventeen," he replied uncertainly.

"What about eighteen, Sergeant?"

But the judge intervened, "I think I have allowed you enough on this line of questioning, Lady Fanshaw. Drop it now, please!"

"Sgt Lucas, on another matter, how do you *know* that the two were naked?"

"Well, er, they were sort of lying there side by side. The boy had bare shoulders and I couldn't see that Mrs Nielsen had any slip on. So, well, I sort of assumed they must be naked."

"You assumed ..., Sgt Lucas. But you did not know? Thank you, no more questions!"

Sam and I wriggled in glee at the wretched man's discomfiture.

Next it was Detective Constable Gallichan's turn on the stand. She was able to add little to her sergeant's evidence, but she was rather more astute at avoiding Lady Fanshaw's traps. Until the end, that is. The latter's final question was: "If you were both so convinced that Mrs Nielsen was committing an offence with the boy, why did you not arrest her there and then?"

The constable was silent and blushed.

"Well, go on, Constable, there must have been a reason? Either you had reason to believe that an offence had been committed, or you did not?"

"You see, well, the blonde one, the lady's son was creating a scene, and, I suppose, you see, I think we both just felt it would be more politic to back off and get further instructions. And anyway I did not know about his age at that stage. And, Jersey is a pretty small place, after all ..." she tailed off lamely.

"Could it be that it was simply that you had precious little evidence of anything having been 'going on'?"

The discomfited DC was silent and blushed again. "So, I think, we can take it then that, in reality, we have no evidence whatsoever that any offence had been committed?"

Again silence.

"So, when did you arrest her, eventually, then?"

"Er, we didn't. When we were preparing to head back up there that evening, we discovered they had already checked out of the hotel, and were booked onto that evening's ferry," she finished miserably.

We could see the amused reaction on the faces of the jury. I drew a large capital H on my note-pad with two oval-shaped balls being kicked over it, and showed it to Sam with a thumbs-up.

We waited expectantly for Inspector Riddle's turn.

But he turned out to be a much smoother operator, at least until the cross-examination.

Mrs Coleman opened: "Inspector, I understand you apprehended Mrs Nielsen in her car for interview at Poole Ferry Terminal. What exactly did she tell you?"

"Let me be precise about this," he began. "My primary concern was to deliver the older boy back to his father. It was he, of course, who had made the original complaint."

"I understand. Did you carry this out?"

"Yes!"

"And the Defendant?"

"In view of the very sensitive nature of the situation, and the unwanted presence of the press ..." (I myself am quite sure Inspector Riddle himself had originally tipped off the scruffy press man.) "I took the decision, on my own initiative, to move the whole show out of Poole and up to the school where matters could be resolved discreetly."

"Most commendable and sensitive, Inspector!" said Mrs Coleman warmly. "To return at last to my opening question: at her interview, did the Accused admit to having indulged in any sort of activity of a sexual nature with the older boy?"

"No, she denied it."

Lady Fanshaw had three questions for him in her cross-examination. "Inspector! Maybe I am being rather slow, but in the previous exchange with my learned colleague, you kept referring to 'the older boy'. Can we be clear about which boy we are talking about, because I understand that they are both the same age?"

"I am referring, of course, to the victim, Ma'am."

"Yes, so much is clear to me. But why do you keep referring to him as 'the older boy'?"

"Well, I mean, he just looks so much ..." the inspector's words ground to a halt.

" ... looks so much older. Quite. Thank you, Inspector: that's a great help, reflecting, I think, what we all feel." To achieve maximum effect, she took her time to sort her papers. "Now, different subject. Who was with the Accused at this interview at the school?"

"Just her solicitor," the inspector replied. "The main reason for moving things up to the school was to give him time to be there to afford her the legal advice to which she was entitled – and to get those two youngsters back to their school."

"And how did she seem, Inspector? At the interview, I mean?"

"Oh, very uncertain and upset."

"So, how much credence would you give to her statement on that occasion?" pursued Lady Fanshaw.

"Oh, I see what you're getting at. To be honest, not too much; she was very upset, and clearly subject to a fair bit of help and prompting by her solicitor." Sam took the note-pad from my hand, found the page with the H symbol on it, and ruefully scrubbed out one of our rugby balls.

After the recess for lunch, the Chief Inspector was called. He had nothing concrete to add and merely confirmed the earlier impression that Inspector Riddle was a fine officer who had conducted a faultless operation – under his own general direction, of course. My father's name, let alone his crucial part in calming the riot, was never even mentioned.

Again, to my surprise and aggravation, the judge called a halt, just as things were getting interesting. While the courtroom was clearing, Sam went over to talk briefly to his mother and cheer her up. Uncle Piers came down and sat beside me: "Not better than thirty/fifteen, I would estimate, Mark! It's easy enough to score points off Mr Plod; and anyway Inspector Riddle did a very tidy job. It now all rests on you, old boy!"

I jumped. "How do you mean, Uncle Piers, on me?"

"I mean, Mr Victim, that's all the witnesses the Prosecution are calling. We are on tomorrow. And the Prosecution is not best pleased that we have stolen their star witness; they think we're mad, and that you are bound to be 'hostile'. You are, of course, Helen's star, Helen's only witness, for that matter – other than herself. Are you up to it? Or are you 'chicken', as they say? Better think about it!"

For a second I felt I was going to be sick. By the time I had recovered myself, Uncle Piers had moved away to talk to Lady Fanshaw. I picked myself up, walked across and interrupted them, "You bet I am, Uncle Piers!"

"Good! Hear that, Jemima? Tomorrow's going to be our day. Have a good night's sleep, Mark!"

Driving back to our B & B from the cinema that evening, I told Sam that I was on the stand next day.

"Yes!" he shook a little balled fist in the air. "I know you'll be fantastic!"

I am not religious, but that night I prayed, as I had never prayed in my life, that I *would* be 'fantastic', not only for Helen, but for Sam and Uncle Piers as well. I dreaded what I had agreed to do, and prayed it would not kill our very precious friendship.

"Call Witness X!" There was a general murmur in the court as I took the stand.

"Before you read from the card, two questions," Lady Fanshaw began. "Are you the so-called Victim in the case against Helen Ann Nielsen?"

"Yes! I am."

"Is your age seventeen?" She hesitated. "Eighteen years old?"

"No!"

Lady Fanshaw feigned surprise: "Oh? What then *is* your date of birth, please?"

I gave it.

Lady Fanshaw paused as though doing the sum for the first time. "That makes you, I calculate, er, fifteen years and three months. Am I correct?"

"Yes!"

"So, last August, you were how old?"

"Fourteen years and ten months." A delicious, comprehending chatter broke out in the court. The judge called for silence.

"Do you have any objection whatsoever," Lady Fanshaw called out above the dying hubbub, "to being *named* as the so-called 'victim' in this case?"

"None whatsoever, Ma'am," I replied firmly. "I would like my side, *our* side of the case to be heard. Moreover, I would like to be allowed to give my evidence on oath. My name is Mark Edward Hallam." Mrs Coleman for the Prosecution stood up. And then sat down again, nonplussed. I understood her anger: not only had I deceived her, albeit passively, up in London, but, worse for her, I had been sitting opposite her for the last three days, and quite certainly she had failed to recognise me, or she would surely have found a moment to come over and acknowledge me.

The judge raised his hand, "Members of the jury, there is nothing in law to prevent the witness from taking the oath. However, as he is under age, you must understand that any evidence he gives on oath must be given no more weight than if he had *not* given it under oath. I hope that is quite clear to everybody. Carry on, please, Lady Fanshaw!"

"And before we start, Mr Hallam, do you understand quite clearly that your name, and everything that you say, may very soon appear publicly in local, and, most probably, in national newspapers?"

"Yes, I can handle that. This case is too important." I paused. "I am full and ready to proceed with your questioning, Ma'am."

"Mr Hallam, do you recognise the Accused?"

"Yes, Ma'am! I have known her for nearly seven years."

Sam, of course, chose this moment, quite unscripted – and I not there to restrain him – to intervene. He stood up on his seat, raised his hand, and spoke out for all the court to hear: "My Lord, I would like – before we start – to sit next to my mother."

It was the judge's turn to be non-plussed: "And who, pray, are you, young man, interrupting my court?"

Without a word in response Sam made his way round to Helen, hopped into the dock beside her and put his arm round her shoulder.

There was an astonished silence. Finally Mrs Coleman rose: "My Lord, I must protest."

Ignoring her, the judge, rather unnecessarily, I thought, repeated his question.

Sam jumped up. "Sir, I am Sam Nielsen, and this lady is my mother. I don't know anything about English Law, Sir, but I have to say that I find it all rather odd that she, supposedly innocent till proved guilty, should be stuck in this dock all on her own, except for these wardens – all just as if she had been condemned already. I would have thought she would have been *seen* to be free until she had been found guilty, or otherwise." Whereupon Sam sat down, to the astonished silence of the hall, many thinking, I imagine, as I did, 'Out of the mouths of babes and sucklings ...'

Clearly wrong-footed, the judge called the two bewigged ladies up, and a brief, inaudible discussion ensued. Then they returned to their stations to hear the judge's ruling: "This is unorthodox, but, for peace and tranquillity, and to expedite this court's business, I am allowing it. But you are quite clear, are you, young man, there are to be *no more* such interruptions?"

Sam nodded. And the case proceeded, orchid and fawn holding hands in the dock.

Lady Fanshaw referred to the first night of our arrival in Studland. "There was a thunderstorm that night, I believe. *Mr Hallam* – she emphasised my title again – would you be willing to tell this court what happened between you and the Accused. We all understand that this is a very delicate matter. Take as much time as you like!"

I had honed my evidence to perfection with Uncle Piers. The two of us had rehearsed it down to the last dot and comma. Over the period of nearly two hours I now described every detail of the development of our love-making, night by night. Very soon, I think I can say, 'you could have heard a pin drop, and there was not a dry eye in the court.' So thrown was the Prosecution by this turn of affairs that Mrs Coleman rose not once to make any point of order. A third of the way through my evidence, I became aware of persistent weeping from a woman at the rear of the court, but was unable to discern its origin.

Throughout, Helen sat silent and detached, Sam beside her, knowing that everything I was saying was being done totally for her.

We rose for a late lunch at the conclusion of my evidence for the Defence. Uncle Piers joined Sam, my matriarch and me. On his arm was my mother. She threw her arms round me: "You dear, dear boy! I promise not to cry any more." I made space for her at the table.

"How long have you been here, Mother?" I asked her rather severely.

"I arrived over last night on the boat from Zeebrugge. But Uncle Piers would not let me see you till you had given your evidence. But finally he has agreed now."

"Well done, Mark!" said Uncle Piers, jovially. "Perfect job! But that's the easy bit, of course; make no mistake! Looking at the judge, though, I fancy he may have been a shade underwhelmed – we may just be going to have a problem with that one. I note that Mrs Coleman is missing out on luncheon and has hidden herself away. You can be sure that she is going to have some hefty questions for you. You and I know what they may be, but the ball is entirely in your court as to how you field them. Remember your rugby defence?"

I grinned. These were catches I had to take and kicks that I could not afford to miss ...

"Have a nip!" He pulled a flask out of his hip-pocket and I felt the unaccustomed liquid burn my throat. "You can only do your best, Mark; we're all rooting for you. Just don't let your heart rule your head!"

That afternoon was the toughest test of my life.

Mrs Coleman set forth to demolish my edifice: "*Master* Hallam!" she began.

I interrupted her immediately: "Ma'am, would it make a great deal of difference to your position if, just for consistency, we were to use the 'Mister' prefix?"

"Mister Hallam, then." She paused. "Mr Hallam, you would appear to be an educated boy, er, man. Would you know, by any chance, the meaning of the words 'paedophile' and 'paedophilia'?"

Before Lady Jemima could stand up, the judge raised his hand: "Mrs Coleman, I don't think that I am going to be at all happy with such a line of questioning."

"Very well, my lord!"

But, as she gathered herself, I decided to respond: "I *would* like to answer that question, my lord." He nodded. "I am a scholar, and my specialist subject is to be English. I am more than old enough fully to understand the meaning and over-tones of both of these words. However, I cannot see that either word can have any relevance whatsoever to the matter under judgement." My pompous voice rose in ill-concealed anger. I looked across at Helen, and I could see Sam making a mark in our note-book.

Mrs Coleman tried again: "I need to ask you: did you ever

make love to the Accused other than in her own hotel room?"

"No! Never."

"I mean, did she ever come to see you in *your* room?"

"No, of course not. It was unnecessary; apart from which it would have meant displacing her son."

"But I thought you told us earlier, under the questioning of my honourable friend, that he condoned your relationship with his mother?"

"Yes, he did. But, well, what a question!" She had suddenly got me angry, but I knew I must not let her get to me.

"All right, we'll leave that. Do you still love the Accused?"

"Yes, of course I do, with all my heart." I felt my anger rising again.

"So, may we know what happens next between you and her?"

Out of the corner of my eye, I saw Lady Jemima rising to intervene. But she was too late: I was too arrogant, just too angry. I cried out: "I fail to see that it is of anybody's concern but mine, Helen's and Sam's. Our feelings for each other are totally private. However, I trust that our former, very normal relationship will resume just as soon as this ghastly dream is over, and the *very day* I reach this arbitrary legal age, in eight months' time, we shall marry." I was shaking with rage.

"No more questions, my lord!" intoned Mrs Coleman, a note of sadness rather than triumph in her voice.

Livid but feeling humiliated, I made my way across to my seat. Sam scuttled back to join me and, for the first time, it was Sam holding *me*, and drying *my* tears. I just blessed that, at that moment, my father was *not* there to witness what I saw as my utter humiliation. As I sat there in my misery, I suddenly caught sight across the court the figure of my mother who was weeping too ...

There was little business left, other than the closing speeches and the judge's summing-up. There had never been any plan by either side, apparently, to call the Accused in her own defence. Certainly Uncle Piers had calculated that I would be a far more reliable witness of her position than she could ever be. Where I had failed him at the last ditch, she would surely have only compounded the disaster.

The judge, needless to say, had adjourned the court early yet again. I made my way over to Helen to say how sorry I was about how I had 'blown it'. All she could do was embrace me, thank me and praise my sincerity, belief in her and for all I had done for her, oblivious of her consequent fate. No one even attempted to intervene in our grief. And Uncle Piers had more sense than to come across and make some comment to me that I would only have interpreted as patronising.

Next morning Mrs Coleman made her closing speech. Her position was transparently predictable. I had simply become infatuated with the charms of an attractive young widow. The accused was demonstrably guilty of having actively brought this about. Vulnerable young men had to be protected from such people. The only solution to this particular situation was to exclude the Accused from all contact with me, specifically, and from society in general until I had grown up into a more clear-headed adult, and age had rendered her less attractive to sensitive young men.

Suddenly, out of the blue, before I could stop him, Sam sprang to his feet next to me, and shouted across the court at her: "You, Madam, are a horrid, spiteful, old woman! May you rot in hell for your wickedness!" and then resumed his seat as if nothing had happened. (This, actually, was a harsh judgement on someone simply carrying out a task, which few would have envied, as sensitively as she could.)

The court was stunned. The judge was so caught off guard, for the second time, that he could only remark quietly, "Carry on, please, Mrs Coleman!".

This remark, too, was embarrassing for her, as all she could say was: "In fact I have concluded, my lord."

Lady Fanshaw did rather better. Her speech was brief and to the point, but got to the heart of the matter. She got up, walked across to the jury and addressed them directly in a manner that made it, unfortunately, a little difficult for the judge to hear unless he listened intently. (And it seemed that he felt no great urgency so to do). Again, I shall attempt to quote her verbatim: "Ladies and Gentlemen of the Jury! Once again, 'out of the mouths of babes and sucklings ...' One way or another the whole truth of this case has been thoroughly aired over the past few days. Fact: despite their age differences, these two people developed a pure and loving relationship, the like of which many of us might envy, first in Studland and then blossoming during a holiday on the honeymoon island of Jersey. Fact: no one has been hurt or damaged, least of all the so-called victim. Fact: they continue to love each other, and no one is going to get hurt if their relationship is allowed to resume. If, together, you decide to invoke the letter, rather than the spirit, of the law in this case, and find the Accused guilty, you risk causing grave, long-term and unnecessary hurt to three people whose relationship is loving, organised, comfortable and, I submit, appropriate. You have it in your power to bless them – or to crucify them. What is undeniable is that the Accused is certainly *not* guilty of 'lewd and indecent conduct'. It would be a travesty of justice to find her guilty of such."

Sam and I grinned at her in total admiration, as she resumed her seat.

The judge's summing-up, on the other hand, was dire. It was entirely in tune with established law and precedent, wholly *out* of tune with the mood of the court. "My task, Ladies and Gentlemen of the Jury, is to guide you towards a correct verdict in law in this wretched case. I have to caution you to cut loose from all the emotional atmosphere that has permeated this place in recent days. You have to ask yourselves: did the accused initiate, or even *countenance*, the development of a sexual relationship between herself and the son that Wing Commander and Mrs Hallam had left in her charge? If you believe she did, then she was indeed guilty of 'lewd and indecent conduct with a minor', and you must find her guilty of such. If, on the other hand, you are inclined to the view that the most eloquent evidence of the Hallams' son was a tissue of lies, then it is open to you to find her not guilty. I appreciate that a proper verdict may be difficult for some of you to come to terms with; I shall be prepared to accept a majority verdict, if I have to. Is there any point in your duty or of law on which you are unclear? No? Then please retire to consider your verdict! If a point does so arise, please do not hesitate to ask for my guidance."

As the jury filed out, Sam and I looked at each other: "Oh Christ!"

He gazed at me through his exhausted, tearful eyes, "That man is a total bastard: he should *not* be allowed to live."

Uncle Piers took us all, including my mother, out into Dorchester for a late lunch. We did not talk much about the case; it had become a taboo subject for the time being. Nobody could see how, after what the judge had said, any jury could eventually find for Helen anything other than a guilty verdict. During lunch Uncle Piers's pager beeped, and he left us to find a phone. He returned with an odd look on his face: "Apparently the jury has come back to ask the judge: if they find Helen guilty, what sort of sentence is she likely to get; and if any, will it be 'suspended'. His basic reply was, predictably: 'Stop asking damned fool questions, and get on with coming up with your verdict!' But obviously they are in a real quandary."

"Tell me, Uncle Piers!" I said, really in an attempt to ease things, "Dorchester is Thomas Hardy's Casterbridge, isn't it? It's just we're doing *The Mayor of Casterbridge* for A-Levels."

He nodded. "But that's not all, Mark: this is where Judge Jeffries presided."

I spluttered into my dessert: "I don't think we want to hear that, do we, Uncle Piers?"

"No!" he agreed, "Somehow, I do not think we do."

We lapsed into silence, my efforts to lighten the atmosphere having failed miserably.

At about 11 a.m. the following day the word was: "We are unwilling to come to your recommended verdict."

"I don't want *my* verdict," the judge exploded. "I have not recommended *any* verdict," he told them. "I just want *your* verdict."

At 3.30 p.m. it was: "We are tied."

Uncle Piers said: "Can't say I blame them: they want the judge to decide it for them. The judge has told them that someone has to break one way or another."

Just after 4 p.m. they filed back. "Mr Foreman, are you agreed on your verdict?"

"No, my lord!" he said angrily. "We are not *at all* agreed with our verdict, but more of us agree than disagree."

"Brave man!" I thought.

But the judge was implacable: "Then how do you find?"

"Technically guilty, my lord!"

There were cries of "No!" from the Gallery. Helen looked resigned and stony-faced. Sam sobbed. And the judge adjourned the court, promising sentence in a week.

There followed a meeting a few days later at Sam's House with Helen, Uncle Piers, Sam, his house-master and matriarch. My mother had returned to Germany. I was not allowed to be there, but learnt subsequently from Uncle Piers what transpired.

He had opened proceedings. "We have to discuss the worst case, I am afraid. Any sentence Helen gets should, in my book, by rights, be 'suspended'. But it just may not be; our man has a reputation for stubbornness and inflexibility. He may decide to throw the whole book at her; and it's a pretty hefty book. Up to ten years even."

Sam immediately interrupted him, "If she goes, I go."

"As you are no longer a babe-in-arms, Sam, old chap, that will just not be possible."

"Just let them try and stop me!" Sam remained icily silent for the rest of the meeting, while contingency plans were discussed.

As the discussions concluded, Sam suddenly stood up and said: "You people can make all the arrangements you like.

One: my mamma is *not* going into any stinking dungeon on her own. Two: during the holidays Mark and I will live in 'Paradise Park', and I will run the business."

Because Sam was clearly in no mood to be argued with, and as he clearly had not noticed that his two statements were incompatible, nobody chose to challenge him.

Uncle Piers tried to cheer things up with, "Well, let's hope it won't come to that anyway." And he and Helen departed.

The judge opened his sentencing at the court seven days later with the announcement that he had agreed to hear a plea in mitigation of sentence.

"Call Master Samuel David Nielsen!" Uncle Piers never ceased to amaze me. I knew this had been within the contingency planning, but Sam had said not a word about this on the journey down from the school with my matriarch.

The Court was deathly quiet as his little figure got up from the seat beside me and padded round to the witness box.

Lady Fanshaw asked him, "Are you Sam David Nielsen?"

"Yes, ma'am!"

"What is your relationship to the Accused?"

"I am her son, her only son."

"May we ask where your father is?"

"He died of cancer three years ago."

"Do you give evidence of good character in the case of the Accused, your mother, Helen Nielsen, entirely voluntarily?"

"Yes, of course I do."

"How did you view the relationship that developed last summer between your mother and Mr Mark Hallam?"

"I was fully aware and supportive of it. I remain so."

"Are you aware of any other relationship that your mother has been involved in recent times?"

"No! There has been no one since my father died when I was eleven. I would know if there had been."

"You say that your father is deceased. In the event that your mother is given a prison sentence in this case, who would you wish to look after you?"

"Mark Hallam."

"You mean, the Hallam family?"

"No, just Mark – with all due respect to the Wing Commander and Mrs Hallam, of course. But Mark and my mamma are the only people in the world who count in my life. And wherever my mother goes, he and I will be. And that includes prison," he added, his voice rising.

"And what would happen to your family motor-racing business?"

"It would be gravely inconvenient, but somehow we would manage. I would have to suspend my education, of course, to keep our business running. My mother would continue to run the book-keeping side from her cell, if she were allowed to, and during the holidays Mark has promised to act as the link and courier between me and my mother." There was a brief intake of breath throughout the court, as the significance of the brave little lad's words sank in. "As I say, we could most sincerely do without the hassle, but it is a challenge that all three of us would meet, if it came to it." Then he added: "And there is Flash to be considered, of course."

"Flash?"

"Flash is my mother's greyhound and body-guard. Like her he is a gentle being; I do not think he will take very well to prison conditions."

"Thank you, Sam!"

The Prosecution had no questions for him. As the tiny fellow stepped down, walked back and settled himself beside me, there was a deathly hush in court. I held his arm. We waited.

The sentence, when it came, was monstrous, unbelievable.

Helen had maintained total serenity and composure throughout the trial. She had seemed almost detached, as if she was watching over some out-of-body experience.

The judge too had seemed increasingly detached from, even disinterested in, the high emotions that were coursing through his courtroom. I do not think he even noticed that both Sam and I, in total disregard of court procedure, had suddenly moved into the dock as guardians on either side of Helen. The police escorts were wise enough not to try to block us. And when Helen rose at the judge's bidding, so did we.

"I am aware," the judge began, "that this case seems to have generated a deal of heat and emotion in this courtroom – and not perhaps quite enough light. Nevertheless I believe the jury's verdict was the right one. The law in this matter is quite clear: juveniles must be seen to be being protected by society from the unwelcome attentions of adults of both sexes until they are old and mature enough to exercise a proper judgement in sexual matters – until indeed they reach the legal age prescribed by the law. While I suspect this court would wish me to pass a suspended sentence on the Accused in this particular case, I have a responsibility to ensure that Mark Hallam, and others like him, are protected from Helen Nielsen until such time as her obvious attractiveness becomes less likely to pose a threat to them. I have no choice but to impose upon her a sentence of five years with the recommendation that, for the reasons I have just given, she serves the full term. This court is adjourned! Take her down!"

There was a stunned silence. Absolutely nobody moved.

Then Helen's voice, quiet, icy and utterly commanding, a voice, that, up till now, had gone unheard, cut across the court: "My lord, all those assembled in this your courtroom know *full well* that you *do* have a choice in this matter, a very wide choice. But if this is your final decision, may God forgive you for your failure, as a human being, to grasp even the fundamentals of this case." She sat down, shaking, while Sam and I hugged her.

The stunned silence was now compounded. For once the judge seemed at a loss. Then Lady Fanshaw slowly rose. But before she could speak, an astonishing thing happened, Mrs Coleman got to her feet, and indicating discreetly to the Defence, said, "My Lord, before this case is actually closed, could my learned colleague and I please speak to you in your rooms for a brief moment?"

The judge nodded, and the three of them moved out of the

room, while a quiet hubbub developed.

I only discovered third hand from Uncle Piers what now ensued in the Judge's Chambers.

Mrs Coleman opened by saying: "My Lord, I have to say, as prosecutor, I have never felt so obliged to express a contrary view, but must now do so in the strongest terms. If you compel Mrs Nielsen to serve a prison sentence, it will be, in my opinion, the gravest mistake. Those two boys have remained totally devoted to her health and welfare throughout the entirety of this affair. I have no doubt whatsoever that they will not be separated from her, and any attempt so to do will incite the press to make a public martyr of her. The whole affair will have a most negative effect on the public's perception of British justice. The one marginal benefit, may I say, might be upon the inmates of her prison where her manifest saintliness will have good effect – always assuming that it does not destroy her first."

"Thank you, Mrs Coleman," the judge responded. "But you have proved to my (admittedly if not entirely to the jury's) total satisfaction that Hallam is infatuated with Mrs Nielsen: the law requires that he be protected from her."

"The law may require that, Sir, but virtually nobody else in that courtroom does. They see a formerly happy family being split by the technicalities of the law. The bottom line is that Hallam looks, and behaves, like an eighteen year old."

"So, Mrs Coleman, what then would you have me do?"

"Confirm your five year sentence, if you must, my Lord, but suspend it!"

The judge spluttered. "And how, pray, do we protect the Victim from the Accused? How will Hallam's parents view such an outcome?"

"We don't, my Lord. And they, I suspect, will not say or do anything: Wing Commander Hallam knows he personally has managed to destroy his relationship with his son, proven, I think, by the fact that not once has he appeared in your courtroom, even as an observer. I think we must quietly accept that this is one case that the Crown Prosecution Service should never have brought. I blame myself for not having acquired a more thorough grasp of the situation before it was brought. 'Fools rush in, where angels fear to tread' – I think that sums up this fiasco perfectly."

The judge pondered, but only briefly. "I hear your comments, Mrs Coleman, and they are noted. I shall, however, not be modifying my sentence. Let us return!"

Lady Jemima Fanshaw now spoke up for the first time, "We shall, of course, be requesting immediate leave to appeal, my lord."

"That is your right, of course, my lady."

When the three gowned and bewigged figures finally returned, the three of us in the dock were sunk in the depths of despair. We could not be convinced that this judge could be moved, and nothing that Uncle Piers could say would persuade us that we would not, all three of us – and we had vowed we would not be split up – be spending that night in prison.

At the judge's bidding to Helen, we two boys rose with her: "Helen Ann Nielsen, I have taken note of certain comments made in your favour by the Prosecution, but the five year sentence is confirmed. Take her down!"

CHAPTER 6

Duo in Defiance

None of us, in retrospect, felt very proud of what happened next: in trying to embarrass the System, we did little more than embarrass ourselves.

What now ensued could only be termed a minor riot. The wardens moved in to separate us, but we blocked them. I was utterly enraged. "Take your grubby hands off her – and off us!"

But Sam, as ever the practical mechanic, had, with amazing foresight, obtained two sets of police handcuffs. In the ensuing hassle he deftly locked one set onto Helen's left wrist and my right, and the second set onto her right wrist and his left. Then, smiling up at the warder, he pronounced: "Right, we're on our way." He then caught sight of our solicitor who was hovering, with a look of total anguish on his face, in the background. I had never seen Uncle Piers in such a state of dither. "We're OK, Uncle Piers," called Sam. "But you had better take the *Volvo* key. My matriarch said she would look after Flashy if the worst came to the worst."

"Right!" our solicitor gestured vaguely. "I am now going down to deal with the press. I will join you down at the nick as soon as I can." He formed his features into what passed for a smile and then fled the ghastly scene.

The warder now got out his handcuff-key and tried to separate us, but failed: "OK, lads, this joke's gone on quite long enough. The key, please!"

"Sorry, officer, no joke, far from it. And I no longer have either key," replied Sam.

"Someone must have it."

"Someone does. But it is not on any one here."

The two warders discussed what to do. Phone calls were made. Finally it was decided to take all three of us down to the local police station. As we bounced along in the Black Maria, I shouted above the noise, "So, where did these manacles come from, Sam?"

He grinned, "When Uncle Piers tipped me off that it was just possible that Mamma could finish up in clink, I enlisted the help of old Jock Halliday in the Mech School. He made me up one set from some plans he had located, and then I copied the second set myself. I bet you can't tell which is mine and which were his. Of course, we put on our own special locking mechanisms. That poor man, when he picks up his *Mirror* in the morning, is going to die of apoplexy ..."

The press were still recording our every move in this drama, and were there set up waiting when we de-bussed at the police station. Here we were given cups of tea while unsuccessful attempts were made to find bolt-cutters. An uncharacteristically flustered Police Sergeant remonstrated, but, in control at last, Sam and I just stayed cool. "Sergeant," I said, "I am sorry we are causing you so much trouble. But we have already told people: 'Where Madam goes, we go'. So I suggest you make arrangements accordingly."

Throughout all this Helen never murmured: utterly shocked by events, she remained in a dream-like trance.

After a lengthy delay we were finally taken, press convoy still in tow, to an Open Women's Prison some thirty miles away. It was now quite late at night, and the Deputy Prison Governor was not best pleased to have been called out to deal with us. On arrival a female warden had been detailed off to take the three of us, linked together, to the loos. It was a farcical operation. To give her due credit, when the Deputy heard what had happened, she could only chuckle. "Play it that way if you like, you boys!" said Carol Retford. "I *could* separate you, but I won't. Right, let's give you some supper and get you all to bed!"

After an excellent Shepherd's Pie and Plum Duff with custard, bearing favourable comparison with our school food, we were led up to a ward in the Prison Hospital, where three beds had been put side by side. Still linked, still half dressed, unable to roll over in our sleep, I can honestly say that three of us spent the worst night of our lives trying to sleep. At some stage I heard Sam speaking with his mother: "Sorry, Mamma, I am afraid this has not quite worked out as I had hoped. I think we'll have to think this one through a bit."

"My son," Helen replied, "you did what you thought was for the best. Prison for me it is – anyway until Uncle Piers can unscramble this awful thing for us."

Next day we had a more than adequate breakfast brought up to us. Then our wily Deputy arrived, "Had a good night, did we?" She had brought up a number of newspapers that were full of the story. We thought the best headline was VICTIM'S NIGHT WITH ACCUSED ... She chuckled again. "Right, what've we got? What's got to be decided now is what we are to do about all of this nonsense. Obviously you boys can't stay here in an adult women's prison, however much I may admire your loyalty and initiative. I was going to recommend we put you into a care institution, but I gather you're both in a similar, equally expensive, care institution already." She continued chuckling at her 'hilarious' joke. "Anyway, I've got in touch with your lawyer, and he is already on his way to help us sort this thing out."

Once she had left, Helen finally took control. "Look, Mark, Sam and I have discussed this thing. What you are both doing for me is truly wonderful, but it can't go on, you know. The law must take its course. This does not seem such a bad sort of place, and so long as you can come and see me regularly, I am sure I can cope for as long as I have to."

So it was that, when Uncle Piers arrived, we had already made up our minds. "Hi, Uncle Piers!"

"My, you fellows are the hottest news in weeks. My people have already started work on your appeal, Helen. So what's to happen here now?"

"Uncle Piers!" I said. "We want you to see the Deputy Prison Governor, and tell her that we will agree to leave on the condition that we can both see Helen here as often as we like. *If* we feel she is being badly treated in any way, we will insist on staying here and generally causing mayhem."

Half an hour later he returned with the assurance that the deal had been struck. Then he took out the two keys Sam had put into his safe-keeping the previous day. Finally, having seen Helen safely to her cell, and had our final hugs, we left with a list of things to bring her the following day.

Back at school we played the modest heroes. Masters and boys alike talked of very little else than about what struck everyone as 'thoroughly senior' goings-on. Even in those comparatively straight-laced times, no one who knew the three of us could see much actually harmful about what had happened, so that everyone without exception was rooting for Sam, Helen and me: the outcome of the trial was being variously described as somewhere between 'ludicrous' and 'plain sadistic'.

The care-group of house-masters, matriarchs, Sam and me, plus Uncle Piers, reassembled in Sam's house and discussed what should be done in the face of this turn of events. "I shall get the Appeal process moving as fast as I can," promised Uncle Piers. "We don't want Helen stuck in that dreadful place a minute longer than necessary; but my worry is that these things always take a long time. Obviously the two boys will need shipping down to the gaol every Sunday afternoon ..."

Everyone nodded and the details were talked through.

Returning on the morrow with my matriarch, with whom we had done some necessary shopping, we re-entered the prison, Sam carrying Helen's suitcase and I her orchid. We were taken to her cell where she was already in animated conversation with Uncle Piers. She seemed resigned and stoical; I felt helpless to do anything. Before we departed, leaving the two grown-ups together, Sam said, "I meant what I said, Uncle Piers: these coming holidays Mark and I go back to 'Paradise Park'. No care institution or staying with relatives for us; Mark is looking after me, and I will be running the business."

"OK, Sam," said Helen, "We'll see, anyway."

"No, Mamma, no 'we'll seeing' this time," retorted Sam with uncharacteristic firmness. "I said that *that* was what was going to happen when questioned in court, and that is what I *insist happens*. Please understand that both of you! Mark and I have discussed it and agreed."

We had not; but I nodded, nonetheless.

I shall not attempt to describe what Helen had to put up with in that gaol, the strip-searching, the din, the vulgarity, the language, the lack of and invasion of privacy, the loss of dignity, and, worst of all, the most unwelcome attentions of the lesbian element: I could write another book about it. Maybe I shall some day, when I have absorbed even the half of it, for, even now, Helen will never speak about it. The entire scene was so totally alien to her nature, her upbringing and her gracefulness.

Although she could show her no favours, for obvious reasons, the Deputy Governor did her very best to ameliorate Helen's situation, and protect her from the worst excesses of that institution. And Helen, in her turn, became an 'angel', a most sought-after and respected counsellor in her own right, for so many of the other female prisoners. Many would turn to her for confidential advice and rely upon her every word. In the giving of herself she retained her sanity.

Two Sundays after her incarceration, Sam's matriarch drove us down to the prison. Flash, whom she was looking after and who had already become a beloved member of the House, came with us. But when we tried to bring him in with us for the visit, the senior janitor refused on the pretext that "It's against regulations, and more'n my job's worth." I asked if we might speak to the Deputy Governor. Reluctantly the man was persuaded to make a phone-call, but then remembered it was her Sunday off. Sadly, we left Flash in the car.

A little unusually, we were allowed to see Helen in her cell, rather than in a big room with dozens of other visitors. She was overwhelmed to see us; our embraces were balm to all sufferings. As always she was immaculately dressed, and

looked as if we had come to visit her in her own home.
"'Fraid they wouldn't let Flashy in, Mamma!" said Sam.

"Oh dear. That *is* distressing. Perhaps the message never got through." But she would say no more on the subject.

Sam's matriarch tried to excuse herself. But we all insisted that she stay. After a while a tray with four cups of tea was brought in by a 'trusty', and we settled down to hear all about her penal experiences. But Helen was strangely reluctant to talk, unwilling to share with us, I suppose, the indignities and privations to which she was being subjected.

We tried another tack. Had she had any good news from Uncle Piers? Nothing specific, the only sure thing was that such things always took time.

"But in the meantime *you* are 'doing time'," burst out Sam.

"You must never forget, Sammy, that, whatever the whys and wherefores, I was found guilty of an offence, was sentenced, and I am now 'doing porridge', as they say round here." Then in a low voice: "Be thankful that at least no one has thought to stop Mark coming to see me!"

We fell silent again. This was all getting very uncomfortable. I began to realise that Helen hated the whole concept of us three seeing her in these alien surroundings.

But Sam was not going to be put off. "Dr Feldmann – he's our new Ancient History man; German, of course – and everyone insists on nick-naming him 'Achtung Feldmann!', which I think is unspeakably rude – but anyway he is absolutely fascinating. He insists that there is no Missing Link in human development. His theory is that man had developed way ahead of us now up until the end of the last Ice Age down on the Plains up to four hundred feet lower than the sea is now. That when temperatures rose, there were these sudden bursts of melt water between about 15 and 11,000 BC from the 9,000 ft glaciers of solid ice, and all these civilisations like Atlantis and in the Bible got flooded, leaving only the less developed folk alive up on the hills. That, if we could go diving down around Cyprus, and Crete and off India and places, we would find the remains of these civilisations from 10–15,000 years ago. I think it's thrilling. I am writing a huge essay on it, and, when I am old enough and have got enough money, I am going to go diving round these islands and find the evidence ..."

As the gush was in full flood, I had watched tears gathering in Helen's eyes. As it ebbed, I walked across and embraced my beloved girl. Sam joined us, and, ignoring his poor matriarch, all three of us wept in unison.

"Oh God, I do miss you both *so much*!" Helen cried.

When we had calmed her down, she looked across at Sam's matriarch: "I am so sorry to involve you in all of this, my dear. Or rather, worse still, *not* involve you ... Now, all of you, thank you for coming; I want you all to go back to school, and forget about me completely for another fortnight."

"Can they bring you anything, Mrs Nielsen?" she asked.

"No! Thank you. But, if I do need something, I will get a message through to whichever of you two wonderful people is bringing the boys next." She paused. "You know, there *is* something. What I would *love* is for you two boys to sing for me next time. I do *so miss* some decent music here. Thank God for Radio 3! And, Sammy, bring your flute!"

We said our goodbyes in a more cheerful mood. "Bring Flashy along again! There should be no problem next time."

For the rest of the term, every Sunday afternoon our respective matriarchs would alternate as ever to take us down in their cars to visit Helen. The Prison staff would always let Flash in, and he was naturally over the moon to greet his true mistress once again.

Helen never seemed anything else but perfectly controlled, although I detected an increasing sallowness in her complexion. Uncle Piers had arranged for her to be sent the firm's books weekly; this, together with the manager's report, seemed to be keeping her partly occupied, partly distracted. But still no positive news came through of her Appeal. For each visit Sam and I had got together a new piece to sing to her, and he would play her his flute. And each time I expected to be told: "No, Mr Hallam, you can't see her any more." But, for some reason, that I never discovered, this never happened. Nevertheless, my every waking hour was still, as before, like moving with an arrow lodged in my back: this pain of our separation was that physical. Indeed, I began to be subject to fits of depression, when I thought of Helen suffering so, when I, after all, was the primary 'criminal'. My passion for Helen had far from died, but I think it was this enforced separation that was the final catalyst for turning that passion into true love. Already I was finding it almost impossible to live without her.

One Saturday Sam appeared in my room out of nowhere. "Mothering Sunday tomorrow, Marcus, I feel a touch of the Rachmaninovs coming on ..." I stared. "Yes, I think it would cheer Mamma up. In fact I know it would. She always said it was her fondest memory of Prep."

I went on staring: we had not sung this piece since that great Prep School Concert.

"I've seen old Argie," continued Sam, "And tomorrow night at Evensong you and I and the whole school are going to sing for her."

"What? Down at the prison?"

"No, idiot! Argie wants us, all the choir, down in Chapel at 9 o'clock tonight for a quick rehearsal. I have already just done a run-through with him; I am still *just* solid enough on the Treble – I think I am going to re-invent myself as a Castrato-with-balls." He grinned. "Malcolm Stannard will be on the organ, and we're going to give it the works. I'll sing the Treble, the boys'll sing the Alto and the Tenor quietish, and you'll sing the Bass, just like we did it before. OK? And we're going to have 'Finlandia' as well, and 'A New Commandment', and 'Hills of the North' with the Pipers, and `St Patrick's Breastplate' to finish."

I nodded, unable to speak; it was a magical idea. "But how will Helen get to hear it?"

"Ah, now, that's the clever bit: Tim Cleaver is borrowing the best sound gear from the Music Department and will record the whole of Evensong live in Chapel tomorrow night."

And so it happened. Word went round. Sam and I – indeed

the whole school – put on the performance of a lifetime for Helen. There was a brief, unnerving silence when the cassette had to be turned over; otherwise it all went brilliantly.

I am not easily driven to emotional demonstration, but as the service progressed, I was smitten with the most dreadful remorse. It was not for Helen any more – all that, for the time being, was spent – but for the total disregard with which I had treated my own mother. After chapel I headed straight for the phone: for once she was there, and she listened wordlessly while I tearfully said my piece and made my peace.

When I had finished, she was silent for a moment, then in a quiet, strangled voice said: "Thank you for all that, Mark. I shall always love you. I must go now." I heard afterwards from my father that 'she went to her room in quite some measure of distress; nevertheless, ringing her was the best thing you ever did, son'.

The following Sunday we took the tape down to Helen. We turned it on, and played her the opening bit of it; but she was so moved that she insisted we stop it and leave it with her to play when she was alone.

It is something she has always treasured. It is rather worn now because, as well as playing it many times herself, it was always played, at the request of the other prisoners, on the last Sunday of each month on the prison tannoy. It brought an hour of utter stillness into their terrible, wasting lives.

I had written a ten page letter to my parents, outlining all that had happened. I explained that I had promised Helen, and her husband on his death-bed, that I would be father to Sam, and so it would be. Finally I made it clear that No, Sorry!, but they would not be seeing me these holidays anyway.

Sam's enterprise never failed to surprise me. One evening he appeared in my room with a flushed look on his face and a

World War 2 flying helmet in his hand, "Guess what? Been flying. Did you see me doing a victory roll over the Coll this afternoon?"

I had not. "Tell me more!"

"Well, I thought it was about time I did something more useful with my wasted life. For weeks now I've been playing with that old Link Trainer in the hut behind the School Laundry, teaching myself to fly. Then, on Old Flighty's suggestion, I cycled across to RAF White Waltham, and persuaded some great guy in the RAF Air Experience Flight section to take me up in a Chipmunk – it's a dual-control trainer with the pupil in the front and the instructor in the back. As soon as we were airborne, he showed me what the plane could do aerobatics-wise: wow, it was absolutely fabulous. As soon as we had landed, I persuaded him to let me do a Circuit & Bump, which I managed OK. On my second flight he let me do everything myself. And then this time he coached me through some aerobatics, and on the way home ..."

I interrupted, " ... You did a victory roll over the College."

Sam nodded, wreathed in smiles. "Bet nobody even saw it. The Squadron Leader said afterwards I was a 'natural' and should apply straight away for an RAF Flying Scholarship. Anyway I am going to get my licence just as soon as I possibly can. Then we can get a plane through the firm, fly it from our own airfield – and I'll be the youngest company chairman with his own plane. That'll show 'em."

"It's fantastic, Sam. You can even fly me home, and land on my dad's airfield in Germany. That really would show 'em."

Thus we planned; thus we dreamt.

At the end of the term Uncle Piers collected us, including Flash, in his *Rolls*, and drove us across to the Nielsen homestead. Despite his reassumed air of jollity, he could not hide his frustration at the time it was taking to get Helen's sentence overturned or suspended.

It was only my second visit to the Nielsens' home. 'Paradise Park' is an old farmhouse with rustic beams on the edge of a little hamlet just back from the main road. We arrived in time for lunch, and Mrs Bardsley was there to greet us. In Helen's absence she had looked after the place faithfully, and had, as ever, a steaming hot meal waiting for the three of us. Sam gave her a hug, and Uncle Piers and I shook her hand warmly. When we had finished our greetings, Flash tip-toed across, stood on his hind legs and gave her a nuzzle. "Yes, Flashy, I have something for you as well." And the two disappeared out to the kitchen.

Once we had eaten, Mrs Bardsley left to catch her bus, and Uncle Piers sat us round the big, oak table in the study. Then he addressed us: "Mark, you are in charge here: in charge of running this house, the provisioning, and above all looking after this rascal here. If things even start going wrong, you first of all get in touch with Bill Townsend down at the factory or, failing that, me. Here is a list of phone numbers. What I have just said is of doubtful legality. So make damned sure you don't cock up, either of you! Otherwise you will make my life even harder than it is already over all of this. Remember to lock the door at night, and do not drink! I know you don't drink or smoke anyway, but you have got to be seen to be whiter than white. Every other Sunday I will be up here to take you over to see Helen. Hopefully you will not get any press attention now, because the story seems to be dead at long last." He paused. "Heavens, this is about the weirdest kettle-of-fish that I have ever had to deal with. Anyway, time to go."

And in a few moments his car was drifting silently away down the drive.

"Right, Marcus," said Sam with assumed pomposity, "get your bag, and I will show you up to your room, Squire!" He led the way up, then pushed open the heavy oak door into Helen's room.

I stood there speechless. This was not the room in which I had seen Sam's father lying on his death-bed. This room was huge, with a magnificent view out across the open fields, but, dominating everything, was their majestic four-poster bed.

Sam patted it proudly. "Yours, old boy. I am diagonally opposite." He was obviously enjoying the look of total uncertainty in my face: for he just smiled, then pushed me down on the counterpane. "'You made your bed, old fellow, now you've got to lie in it.' as somebody once said, I believe." I looked up almost pleadingly: "And Mark, don't expect to come sleeping with me, that's just not on, you know." He chuckled at his jest. Then he went over to his own room, and I soon heard him playing some of his favourite pop records.

I sat there for a long time just staring out. Then I took off my shoes and lay down on the bedspread, wondering if I should lie on the left or right hand side as I pictured Helen beside me. "Oh, Helen!" I prayed. "Help me to do this thing right! Please!"

Soon I fell asleep, not waking till Sam was beside me.

"Come on, mate! Time you cooked me my supper!"

I knew Sam could cook as well as I could, but realised that he was anxious to get the role-playing right. I fried some bread on the Aga, heated up some tins of baked beans and sausage. We washed these down with some Coke, and Sam pronounced the meal a culinary disaster: "Where were you dragged up, for heaven's sake? Have we learnt nothing at school? Gor-blimey!" But he did the dishes with good grace, notwithstanding. Then we watched some TV, and went to bed.

I slept like a log in this temple of my goddess. When I finally awoke, I was attracted to the rear windows by mechanical noises coming from outside. I looked out, and saw Sam had got out the *Saab* and was tinkering with it. He looked up.

"Hurry up, Mark! Get some breakfast down you! I've had mine. We're off down to the works."

I dressed and ate in a hurry, Flash hopped in the back of the car and then we were off. After a few minutes Sam glanced across to me, "OK? Couldn't take the *Volvo*, still can't reach the pedals properly."

It was only at this point that I realised, with dawning horror, that Sam was driving under-age, unlicensed and uninsured. I decided to say nothing, for the present. We arrived safely at the barrier to enter the works. Paul, the gateman, immediately recognised Sam and reached in to shake his hand with huge enthusiasm. We parked up, and Sam led me in.

He introduced me to Bill Townsend, the works manager; then spent an hour introducing me to everyone, and showing me all the exciting development projects that were under way. Quite clearly they all adored Sam. Finally I was left in Bill's office, overlooking the shop-floor, with a cup of tea.

About half an hour later, Bill returned and he and I had a lengthy talk, and we were soon on first name terms. Finally I raised with him the matter that was uppermost in my mind.

"Yes, Mark, we have got to keep that lad safe and out of trouble. In another year he will be ready to start racing for us – and making money for us. We certainly don't want any run-ins with the law in the meantime. No *more* run-ins, shall we say?" He smiled, then told me what he had in mind.

When we got back to 'Paradise Park' much later, and Sam had parked the *Saab* next to the *Volvo* in the garage, I reached across and took the keys out of the ignition. "Mine, I think, Sam!"

He rounded on me: "What the hell do you mean by that?"

"Come inside! You know *exactly* what I mean, and we need to talk." I started to get supper ready. "You remember what Uncle Piers said, Sam? You are a brilliant driver, no messing. But you cannot, will not, are not allowed to, and I will not allow you to drive any car on public roads again until you are licensed and insured."

Sam was deathly silent, as he watched so many of his plans going down the pan.

Finally he got up, walked to the door, stopped, looked over his shoulder, and said: "You, Mark, are a total bastard, and I hate you like I have never hated anyone before, that judge not excluded." He paused. "And now I've got a job to do."

He went outside to the workshop, and then reappeared with a heavy tool-box and one of two identically sized metal signs that he had brought back with him from the works. On one sign was embossed the word LOST; on the other REGAINED. With these he descended to the front gate.

When he returned some fifteen minutes later, he had obviously been crying. The old PARK sign he threw in the bin; the REGAINED sign he propped up on the kitchen dresser for a future occasion. Then he washed his hands and sat down silently at the oak table till supper was ready.

"Good idea that, Sam! Just so people jolly well *know*," I observed quietly.

He nodded.

No further word passed between us in the room during that meal. Then he went out to watch the TV in the drawing-room, leaving me to clear up. In due course I joined him in front of the television. Still not a word. When his programme was over – 'The Professionals', I think it was – I said I was going to bed. As I went up, he followed me up the stairs.

"Mark! Come and see my room!" He led me in. I was open-mouthed at the artistry of it, his own watercolours of Swedish landscapes, flutes and other wind instruments hanging from the walls, and over his bed a gallery of hunky Swedish men.

"They *are* rather dishy, aren't they?"

I nodded, not feeling particularly qualified to comment. But what was holding me spellbound was the life-size 'David' sculpture standing against the wall opposite the end of his bed. I knew Sam sculpted, but here was a very passable copy of the 'David' statue in Florence. But it was that head: it was not the David head, but somebody else's, whom I could swear I recognised. "I am sure I've seen him somewhere ..."

"You have, often." Sam smiled impishly. "He's in my House. He used to live in my dreams – and just occasionally in my bed, I have to admit."

"I know. Earl of Gorringe. In the year above ours."

"Yes, Johnny Gorringe and I have been close ever since I arrived."

"Oh, Sam! You're incorrigible. What are you going to do with it – once the infatuation dies?"

"I shall store it here. He has already seen it, and was dashed chuffed with it, actually. I promised to leave it to him in my will. Should stand well in the baronial hall." He chuckled wistfully. "Maybe I shall send it to him as a wedding present – to remind him of his misspent youth ..."

"I doubt if his wife-to-be will thank you."

He threw himself down on the bed, and looked up at me, appealing, apologetic. "Sorry, Mark, I am the bastard. You are quite right, of course. I will take the bus in tomorrow, like all ordinary mortals. Our first row, already! Can you ever forgive me?" I could see he was about to cry, and knelt down on the floor next to him. Then I held him while he sobbed. "Oh, Mark, I do *so* miss my Mamma. How could those meanies just take her away from us like that?"

I got up and sat next to him, and we contemplated the bleak future in silence. Finally he looked at me with his mournful eyes. "Would you mind cuddling me just a *bit* tonight? I don't know if I can face things alone at the moment."

I considered. "OK, Sam, why not? *Of course* we can cuddle."

Human love takes many forms. The expression of love-sharing between men is a gift granted to a few, alarming to most, reviled by many. Such love was never something I could ever have quite got used to: I am just not made that way. Yet nothing that I ever did with Sam ever disgusted me. On our first occasion I had been little more than a bystander of his attentions, aware though I was of the intensity of his genuine love that flowed beyond lust.

On this second occasion with him as partner, we were both in desperate need of the mutual love and support that such sharing could offer. I believe I was able to snatch from it at least an inkling of the eroticism, in addition to the love, generated by his caressings. Our love-making that night – I choose to call it that, for such I know it truly was – was lengthy and dream-like, and dissolved the soreness of our earlier, petulant row. And in offering my love to Sam, I felt I was as close as ever I could be to his beloved, deserted, suffering mother in her dank prison-cell.

It was the last time we ever so shared together. As he lay between my parted legs, having finally spent his all upon me, I gently stroked his golden locks with one hand – and the cheeks of his little bottom with the other – a bottom that only a few years ago was so nearly disfigured by a headmaster's brutish cane. I gave voice to my thoughts: "Caning is so wicked, I feel."

"Um ... I gather some masters found it quite a turn-on ..."

I had not thought of that. I stroked his bottom again. Finding a couple of tiny pimples, I said to the head beside mine – very, very quietly so as not to spoil the moment for him, "Do you know what I think, Sam? I think you have got some spots on your bum."

He twitched before replying. Then he sighed: "As I said before, Marcus, you are a total bastard. Not only have you just ruined my holidays, you have now discovered my most guilty secret. No Nielsen is *ever* subject to spots. Yet I have, as you have so tastelessly pointed out, grown spots on my ass. I'll be getting them on my face next – *and* we have no matriarch here to minister to same. In the Middle Ages they would have solved the problem with the cat-o'nine-tails." He was silent for a while, reluctant to end our time together. Then: "I'll let you into another secret too, which is really going to make your day: there is this new typist down at the works that I have just the beginnings – no more than the beginnings, you understand – of a hankering for. Tomorrow I am going to break the habit of a life-time and try a bit of what, I believe, is called by you hairy old gentlemen a 'chat-up line'. And my nice young friends up there on the wall above us may have, sadly, to be relegated to the archives. Maybe."

"Sam, that is just wonderful," I replied, genuinely delighted. "But, look, I am bound to advise you as guardian and mentor, what you seem to be proposing is *just not legal*. I have it on good authority that, if one so young as you, should seduce a lady, *she* could well get locked up."

"She? Locked up? I've never heard such nonsense."

We chuckled at the supreme irony of it.

Then he sighed nostalgically, "Yes, all the men in my life, ninety per cent of them anyway, have been a whole lot of fun, and I like to think no one's got hurt; but that, I suppose, is what growing up's all about. All good things eventually come to an end or just move on." We lay there a while longer thinking about all that had happened.

Finally he said briskly, "Thanks for that, mate! I feel a whole lot better now, and able to face this wicked place: let us shower off these gorgeous bodies of ours, and you can sod off back to your own bed, while I rearrange my fantasies for this brave new world of blondes and boobs. I may well need guidance."

At breakfast next morning I found Sam sitting at the kitchen table, moodily stoking his Muesli. I knew what was on his mind: "You could, of course, always run ... or cycle ... and soon you'll be old enough to get a provisional licence for a *Vespa* ..."

"Don't rub it in, Mark! Me on a scooter? Pah! Bloody dangerous things. When's this bus anyway?"

I looked at my watch. "There was one at 07:40; there'll be another at 09:40. So you've got a bit of time yet."

He was silent for a while. "So, what's *your* great plan for the day?"

"I shall hold a long-term strategy meeting with Mrs Bardsley," I replied with mock pomposity, "So that we don't get under each others' feet. Then, at the risk of seeming incredibly dull, I shall settle down to some serious studying."

Sam continued to gaze miserably out of the window. Then, slap on cue, this huge classic 1940's black *Humber* sidled up the drive. Sam stood up and gawped: "Christ! That's one of ours, and that's Peter Metcalf at the wheel." It stopped, and Mrs Bardsley stepped out of the back seat like royalty. Sam turned to me: "This is your doing, isn't it? You *are* the ultimate total bastard, after all: you put me through all of that and never breathed an effing word."

I smiled, enjoying his discomfiture hugely, "Your carriage awaits, Mr Chairman. Shall I keep Flashy here? He needs his run." The latter was up on his feet in a trice.

I watched as the tiny, now not so tiny, figure in his team works overalls stepped proudly aboard, and was chauffeured off to his place of work. Things, I felt, were going to be all right – eventually, anyway.

Mrs Bardsley made us both a cup of tea, and we sat down to agree demarcation arrangements.

CHAPTER 7

Aftermath

By the special dispensation of my school and Carol Retford, the Deputy Prison Governor, I was married in the Prison Chapel to Helen Nielsen ten months later in the holidays following my sixteenth birthday. Uncle Piers gave away the bride; Sam was our best man. My parents, having finally given their consent, attended the wedding, as did our respective house-masters and matriarchs, together with many other friends and well-wishers, including Lady Jemima Fanshaw and Mrs Anne Coleman. Lord Justice Percival Phipps declined his invitation with regret – prior commitment to his bees, maybe? – so it was a supremely auspicious occasion.

In response to Helen's request the Prison Governor had also agreed to the erection of a marquee in the prison grounds, and, at Helen's further request, to the attendance of all the prisoners and staff. Despite the shortage of alcohol, which was confined to a glass of champagne each, it was a wild affair in every sense.

We thought it inappropriate, on Uncle Piers' advice, with Helen's Appeal coming up, to ask to be allowed to consummate our nuptials within the prison walls – to the disappointment of all the other prisoners amongst whom it had been a major talking point.

Two months after our wedding, Helen's Appeal *was* allowed. The unserved portion of her sentence was suspended – though she was never pardoned.

Three hundred and eighty-seven days she had served.

This time we had a further celebration with a slightly smaller and more select group in the grounds of Sam's House at the School. Uncle Piers was clearly mightily relieved that

135

the whole saga had finally come to a fair conclusion. As he commented to me at the time: "That bloody man. Did the legal system no good at all. Caused untold misery and inconvenience. And cost the tax-payer, of course, an absolute fortune to achieve nothing positive whatsoever. Thank God it's all over."

It was the start of half-term. So we set off in the *Volvo* once again, Helen, Sam, I and Flash, for our beloved Chalet Hotel in Jersey. Aunt Maude had recently died, and there was now a rather unsightly hole where her little wooden house used to be – prior to the ground being taken over by the Chalet.

And there, finally, in the same rooms where it all had started, seemingly aeons ago, our marriage was finally consummated. To be more specific, Helen and I sat all evening after supper on our own together looking out to sea saying very little and watching the lights twinkling along the French coast. I opened our bottle of champagne, and when we had finished it, I said, "Come along, Mrs Hallam, time for bed."

We undressed one another, and stood naked in the moonlight. Finally she said, "Oh Mark! It has been so long. You can just have no conception how badly I have missed you." She was silent for a while. Then: "Please. I don't want actually to *do* anything yet. I just need you to hold me."

Very quietly we got into bed. I put my arms around her; then slowly she began to shake, and then she wept and wept, as all those days of hurt drained from her.

Finally we slept.

I had asked for another orchid to be delivered to her room. As the sun rose, I pulled back our bed clothes. As orchid and I rose together, as once we had before, Helen breathed me a welcoming smile: "OK, you gorgeous monster, do your worst! Now I *am* ready, at last I really am ready for you." And we sank together into the most rapturous love-making beyond anything that I had ever experienced with Helen before – or since.

So pre-occupied were my wife and I with catching up on our lives, that we had paid scant attention to Sam that previous evening. We were a little startled, therefore, when we knocked on his door a few hours later, as we stirred ourselves for a late breakfast, that there should be no answer. And not only no answer, but, when we looked in, we found his bed had not been slept in. On the bed, however, was a note in his familiar, neat scrawl: "Worry not, aged parents! – or perhaps you should (?) ... See you down at breakfast! – always assuming I survive the night. 'Such games that lovers play ...'"

We hurried down to the dining-room. There at our table sat our, or rather Helen's, sixteen year old son in animated conversation with an incredibly pretty Eurasian girl in her early twenties.

Sam stood up, his eyes piercing right through me with a look of exquisite triumph: "Hi, Mamma! Hi, Marcus! Did you two love-birds both have a restful night? I, if I may, would now like to introduce you to Mahjong, my lady of many months. You may not have met her before but she is now in charge of designing our new racing-team uniform. And, well, we just seem to agree on a lot of things ..."

Epilogue

As an afterthought, I might mention that Sam taught me to drive on the works' perimeter. He duly passed his own driving test a week after his seventeenth birthday, and a month later I passed mine as well.

Sam made Captain of Swimming and Master of the Beagles but, having achieved his two A-Levels (just), felt he had more useful things to do with his time than go up to university. To be accurate, he spent just under one term studying Engineering at one of the so-called 'new' universities – a former Technical College – finally walking out of one lecture, telling his tutor just what he thought, packing up his stuff and driving straight back to the factory. That evening he told us: "I've learnt absolutely *nothing* at that place I did not know already, and I reckon I can learn a hell of a lot more from our own people here." We had more sense than to disagree with him.

Under his and Helen's helm the firm thrived. His days were spent either in or under racing cars, developing new and more exciting models, not only of the metal/plastic sort, but of the female variety as well. Every year he would fly us over to Jersey in the firm's little jet for a sacrosanct reunion holiday – until finally the Chalet Hotel closed. (Our beloved refuge has recently been knocked down and replaced by a very swanky luxury apartment block.)

I concluded my school career as Head of School, Elector of that aristocracy that maintains discipline within the school, and Captain of Rugby. I also left, of course, with the signal distinction of being, I believe, the only boy ever to enter the married state while still *at* the school. I then went up to

Cambridge where I achieved my 'First', and am now a Fellow and a Professor of English – holding the law in some contempt, as I do, I felt I could never take it up as a profession. I am also on the board of Rugby Football referees.

Helen still runs the money side of *Nielsens Racing & Car Design*. The adorable baby boy and girl we adopted in Sri Lanka are now both at university.

Appropriately, in memory of the husband that was so ruthlessly snatched from her, she now does much good work with the *Orchid Cancer Appeal*.

Early in our marriage Helen persuaded me that the essence of life was true forgiveness. At her insistence she compelled me to face up to and make the journey I so much dreaded, that one to my parents' home in Germany. Initially, it was a brittle reunion for all of us, but, on the third evening, Helen and my mother went out, leaving my father and me alone together; we were able to talk long into the night, and finally settled our differences. Eventually, I was able to come to understand that the disastrous action, that my father had taken, was only what any caring parent *should* rightly have done. The difficulty had been that we, both of us, had utterly failed to communicate throughout my early life: it was this total breakdown that had generated a run-away situation. And once the law had intervened, things had swiftly moved beyond his capacity to remedy them or to put the clock back.

My parents and I still function on different wave-lengths, even though my father is now far gone into his retirement, but at least we can now communicate civilly, with mutual respect and with comparative ease.

Helen also insisted on writing a brief letter of forgiveness to Lord Justice Phipps. He acknowledged it equally briefly, but what he made of it, we shall never know. In fact Uncle Piers, who is unfortunately now not very well at all, rang me recently to say that he had just read of the death of Lord Justice Phipps. Eighty-seven he was – but then he had already in my view reached an over-ripe age when he so casually sentenced the lady whom I loved. I wondered whether his declining years were troubled in any way? Somehow I rather doubt it – there are 'none so blind as those who will not see ...'

Colonel the Honourable Gervaise Lockhart died 'on active service' in the 1st Gulf War. The circumstances thereof were never made entirely clear to us. Helen had kept in occasional touch. A very lonely man, he had never re-married and had continued to drink somewhat excessively. The latter part of his career had taken him into the service of the Gulf States, where he had distinguished himself on a number of occasions, and been decorated. After the Iraqi occupation of Kuwait he had volunteered to lead a small band of infiltrators back into Kuwait City during the build-up to the Alliance invasion. A week before the party was due to go in he had been inoculated with the standard cocktail of drugs. Forty-eight hours later he was dead: the cause, officially, was liver-failure – which was, we supposed, the truth, if only part of the truth.

Helen and I continue to do our best to ensure that Sam attains a ripe old age, as he hurtles around the world's skies and racing tracks. Occasionally we go to a race-meeting to spectate, but, while the atmosphere is addictive, it terrifies both of us. At least, despite the pressure, Sam has never taken up smoking.

We parted with the so-called 'David' statue over ten years ago now. Things can happen in the most mysterious way. One Friday evening Sam appeared from the office for supper with a wry smile on his face: "Remember Johnny Gorringe? He's coming by for his statue. I could do with a spot of help after sups to get it out of the shed and give it a clean. Mamma, I hope it's OK: I asked him and his mother over for lunch tomorrow."

"Mother?" I queried.

"Yup!" But he would not be drawn further.

We dusted the sculpture off, cleaned him up and stood him in the hall with a sheet over him.

Promptly at 12.30 p.m. next day a very smart *Bristol* coasted up the drive, and out stepped a most attractive lady about my own age and a callow youth of about fifteen.

"So, who's the kid, Sam?" I whispered.

"That's Johnny Gorringe Mk 2," he whispered back.

"Looks very like his Dad when I knew him at the same age."

"Biblically, you mean?" I ventured.

"Shush, Mark! Enough said; don't want to frighten the servants, do we?"

The Earl of Gorringe seemed a fairly self-assured sort, and introduced his mother as Fiona. "I'm Johnny, by the way."

Both Helen and I were totally mystified, but clearly Sam was enjoying his joke hugely. I poured the drinks, Helen checked the beef in the oven, and then settled down with us in the drawing-room. We all reminisced at length about the old school, but once the joint was on the table, carved and served, Sam turned to the object of their journey: "Right, young sir! Now you can go ahead and tell these good people your amazing tale."

"Pretty simple really," said the youngster. "Up till six months ago I was Johnny Pelham, son of Fiona Pelham, single mum late of the Parish of Ely. I am now the Earl of Gorringe. You go on, Mum!"

"Well! Some seventeen years ago I was taken on as PA to the Earl of Gorringe. He was a bachelor, and one thing led to another, and some eighteen months later this fine young man was on the way. There was no question of our getting married, but the earl very properly decided to do the decent thing, to pension me off and to pay for our upkeep and the lad's – his lad's – education. We saw absolutely nothing of him, though, until his solicitor called us to his hospital bed. Apparently he had picked up a malignant malaria bug in Zimbabwe, and he was anxious to meet his only son. We saw him just three days before he died. He told us that Johnny here would inherit his title, but, much more important, he said, was that he should claim as part of his inheritance the Nielsen statue of himself. So here we are!"

"But I see you have covered it up, though?" queried the boy.

Sam and I looked at each other. Finally I broke the silence. "As you said, pretty simple really. He is, er, rather less than dressed for the occasion, and, well, there are only two people here who can vouch, shall we say, for his credentials: one is your mother here and the other is, er, Mr Nielsen. But we have no doubt at all that he will stand well in the baronial hall. As soon as we've eaten, we men will wrap him up against the cold and install him across the back seat of your old banger out there. Were you about to say something, Sam? ..."

Flash moved on at the end of his little life. He was followed by a succession of loyal colleagues, as we became an established retirement home for five year old greyhounds. After the kids had gone to boarding school, Helen took to breeding the elegant little creatures, and as each litter of puppies staggered to their feet, I was reminded of that night so long ago when Sam rescued the fawn fleeing from the woods in the thunder-storm – and had nearly been beaten for his troubles.

As I close, the most exciting news of all is that Sam has just e-mailed us from Buenos Aires in high excitement to announce, at the ripe old age of forty-five, his engagement ... I am to be his Best Man, and together we will sing our Rachmaninov, and can the kids be bridesmaid and usher? and can we have the Reception, please, at 'Paradise Regained'? and the *Humber* is to be pulled out of retirement; and has he left anyone off the guest-list at Attachment? and could Helen and I just pop over to Jersey, on their behalf, to reconnoitre a worthy successor to the dear departed Chalet Hotel? and is The Book finished? – with nothing chopped out? – and what will you call it? ... and ... and ...

I e-mailed back to *sam@hotrubber.com:*

> *Sam!*
>
> *Muchos congracias, compadre! Once again you have managed to get your mother all upset. We here are all, of course, over the moon; and the answer, naturally, is Yes! in every department – but are you still confident about those top notes?*
>
> *Marriage, don't forget, is about the begetting of our grandchildren as well as the comforts in your decrepit old age. So*

the critical question now arises, old friend: after all these dissolute years, are you sure you are really up to this new challenge? Remember Bolsover Mi in Divinity? – can your heart/loins match his record?

Yes, The Orchid and the Fawn is ready for your approval. Unexpurgated!

Advise preferred date of nuptials; also your ETA!

Can't wait. Best love.

M & H

Until they both fetch up here, we shall have not a clue as to the nationality of his intended, but we have no doubt at all that she will be an absolute stunner – and surely a fine mother, too.

And so, all is very well.

2004 MEH

About the Author

Christopher Davey is a Jerseyman. His grandfather and great grandfather ran a boarding school in Jersey. His father was a general and a Jurat of the Royal Court of Jersey. Christopher was educated at Beaudesert Park School, Eton College and Jesus College, Cambridge, where he studied Modern Languages. He stroked the winning 1960 Eton Ladies Plate VIII at Henley, and was then President and Stroke of the winning 1964 Boat Race Crew. While serving with the 2nd Royal Tank Regiment in Rhine Army and Northern Ireland, he started hot air ballooning as an adventurous training sport in the Army. In 1975 he flew the giant *Heineken* balloon with Don Cameron, the manufacturer, and a French count, from Yeovil in Somerset to Angers in France on a record-breaking flight. In 1981 he also completed with Flight Lieutenant Crispin Williams the first North Sea west to east flight from Hull to the Moselle in the same balloon re-christened *Crest Warrior* after the sponsor. His first book *Zanussi: Transatlantic Balloon* was published following the first nearly successful trans-Atlantic flight (from St John's, Newfoundland, to the Bay of Biscay) which he undertook with Don Cameron in 1978. This experimental balloon, which ruptured in mid-ocean, was the first combination Helium/Hot Air balloon, subsequent developments of which culminated in 1999 in the successful Piccard-Jones round-the-world flight.

Back home now in Jersey, Christopher interviews, proofreads, sings and acts, and pursues environmental causes. In 1979 he married Debbie Cooper, his Canadian wife from the St John's adventure, who sings and acts with him. Their son, Dominic, is a Cavalry officer; their daughter, Colette, is a medical student, training to be an Army doctor.